TWO FOR THE ROAD

An Adam Fraley Mystery

HENRY HOFFMAN

TWO FOR THE ROAD
Copyright © 2020 by Henry Hoffman

ISBN: 978-1-68046-929-5

Melange Books, LLC
White Bear Lake, MN 55110
www.melange-books.com

Published in the United States of America.

Cover Design by Ashley Redbird Designs

To Jessica

———

Special thanks to Barbara Whelehan for her assistance in the preparation of the manuscript.

"Vice is a monster of so frightful mien
    As to be hated needs but to be seen;
    Yet seen too oft, familiar with her face,
    We first endure, then pity, then embrace."

          — ALEXANDER POPE, *AN ESSAY ON MAN*

CHAPTER ONE

April 1997

THE PARAMOUNT LESSON ADAM FRALEY LEARNED EARLY ON IN the private investigation business was to place a premium on case selection. Much like personnel hiring, you want to make sure you take on the right case, just as you would the right person, lest you end up drowned in disappointment and endless damage control. Fortunately, he had thus far successfully managed this aspect of the business. First, by hiring Tamra Fugit several years ago as his office manager. Secondly, by relying on her knack for making the right choices. Still, no selection system was foolproof. As an old boss of his was fond of saying, "You can only ride horses so many times before you get bucked off one." Consequently, the admonition was always in the back of his mind when he and she met for their regular Monday morning caseload review.

"What's on the agenda?" he asked from a visitor's chair positioned in front of her desk.

"Two cases—one for you and one for me," she said, working her desktop computer.

He halted in mid-motion the sip of coffee he was about to take to look askance at her.

She swiveled her chair to face him. "I've assisted you in nearly every case we've taken on since I was hired here, Adam. And thanks to your generosity, I will soon own half of the business. No better time for me to start taking half ownership of some of the cases, don't you agree?"

"By ownership you mean taking to the street---the actual gumshoe part."

"Yes...surveillance and tracking."

"Who's going to take care of the office end of it while we're out gumshoeing?" he asked, carefully setting his coffee cup on her desk.

"Think of it this way," she replied. "As with the modern family, the mother sometimes stays home to tend to the house and kids while the father is at work. Conversely, the husband stays home while the working wife takes to the road. We are destined to become a family business, are we not?"

"You're looking terrific today," he abruptly said to the woman who would have to be subjected to prolonged physical duress, say like an extended hike through the Mohave desert, to look bad---the woman, by the way, he happened to be betrothed to. But for her presence, the Adam Fraley Private Investigations office could best be described as nondescript, he opined.

"Do you realize your auburn hair, beautiful green eyes, and bright yellow dress offset very well the dull cast of this office?" he continued.

"You're digressing," she said. "Or are you stalling?"

"Okay, what are the two?" he asked in resignation.

"The first is for you," she said, sorting through some notes on her desk. "I received a call from a woman by the name of Carmen Rivera. She was calling from Bogota, Colombia, where she lives. She has a son by the name of Manny who is attending Coastal State College here. She and her husband have not heard from Manny in over a month.

Normally, he checks in with them at least once or twice a week. He lives in an off-campus home which he shares with another student who, for whatever reason, claims no knowledge of his whereabouts."

"She's contacted the cops?"

"Yes, and received the standard reply. Since he is an adult and there is no evidence of foul play, they will not get involved at this point."

"We should send the department a thank you note, considering how much business that policy of theirs generates for us. You have the address for the kid?"

She again scrambled through the notes on her desk, picked one out and handed it to him. "Here you go."

"Before we get started, how are we handling the fees? It's not like we have a history of job requests from overseas on which to draw from. In fact, we have no history of it...right?"

"Correct," she said. "However, if we do take the case, she will wire us a down payment upfront with the remainder to follow once we have concluded our investigation."

"What do you think?" he asked. "Legitimate?"

"She spoke in a very cultured voice and with a mother's concern. My sense is the Rivera family could very well be one of the five percent of the populace who control the wealth of the country."

"Five percent...is that a fact or your opinion?"

"It comes from a former roommate of mine who spent a half year in the country."

"Doing what?"

"Studying the Colombia rainforest region."

"For what?"

"Six course credits," she cracked. "She was in a study abroad program."

"Well, it's not likely we're going to break the parents financially," he said. "And the second case---the one you've put a claim to?"

Tamra glanced at another note on her desk. "I received a call from a man named Mickey Riley. He says his sister went missing about four weeks ago. He wants us to find her."

"Let me guess...the cops don't want to get involved because she is an adult and there is no evidence of foul play."

"You got it."

"So, does Mickey have any idea where his sister might be?"

"With her husband somewhere, he says."

"And that's a bad thing?" Adam asked, no doubt repeating the same question the cops asked the brother.

"According to Mickey, the husband, himself, is a bad thing...a very bad thing. Apparently, his sister has become a virtual prisoner of her husband, to the point he won't even let her out of the house. A control freak, to say the least."

"So, you aim to free her?"

"I aim to find her. It's up to the brother to free her. He's coming in for a meeting this afternoon. I should know more then, including where would be a good place to start looking for her. Meanwhile, your mother called. She'd like to know if we want a wedding planner. If so, she knows of a good one."

"We've already decided we don't need one, don't you remember?"

"I certainly do, but apparently you failed to pass that bit of info along to her."

"I'll tell her when we finish with these two cases," he sighed, perturbed by his oversight.

"You know, this will be a good time to go on the road," he followed. "Noelle will be on her school-sponsored camping trip. We should be home by the time she returns."

"If all goes well," Tamra responded with a deadpan expression.

Adam leaned across the desk. "I have a proposition for you. How about we flip the cases? You trail after the missing student and I chase after the missing sister? You know how volatile these simmering domestic situations can get. They're invariably about some demented guy's passion to control another, usually a helpless woman, like the one you describe in this case. The moment you

4

show up, you become a threat to take away that control. Needless to say, he's not going to like that at all."

"Are you worried for my safety? Would you rather I go chasing after porch poachers...sit in the car for hours on end waiting for a home delivery to be stolen? We still have one of those requests on the back burner waiting for a decision."

"No, I'm not worried for your safety. It's the safety of the captive wife's husband, I'm worried about," he joshed, rising from his chair to give her a quick kiss, followed by a longer one, before heading out of the office. "Before you leave, I have two other items to run by you," she said, halting his movement.

"Okay...the first?"

"Harold Jenkins, the attorney from The Justice Brigade called. He wants to know if you'd like to meet with him regarding the merger idea that he discussed with you over the phone a while back."

Adam slipped back into the chair, indicating it was a subject requiring immediate attention. "What do you think?" he asked of her.

Tamra gave a slight shrug. "I remember you mentioned the idea at the time. Run it by me again."

"They're interested in bringing us into their fold via some sort of a partnership, whether it be a corporate takeover, merger, or retainer-type arrangement. Whatever it takes to get us on board."

"A big operation like theirs? What for?"

"Law firms have a need for tracking missing persons or conducting background checks, as you well know..."

"Yes, we've conducted several for them recently," she interjected.

"Right, and apparently they liked the results. The Justice Brigade is one of those young, aggressive, fast-growing firms looking to gain a leg up on their competition. It's not like they don't have many law firms to compete with."

Tamra flashed a look of surprise. "By doing their own detective work?"

"My guess is they're planning to become a one-stop shopping operation, so to speak."

"What's in it for us?"

"Well, it could mean a steady work flow, which is no small matter. Looking down the road a way, there's Noelle's college tuition costs looming on the horizon. Right now, we're operating at a small profit margin, enough to keep us afloat for the time being. However, as you and I have discussed, we've reached the stage where we're either going to have to raise production or raise prices. I have a hunch joining forces with the Justice Brigade would lessen our office management burden significantly. Taking on the bulk of our paperwork would be an insignificant addition to their overall workload. Doing so would allow us to concentrate on the detective work."

"You're making it sound like—what do they call it in the business world—a white knight coming to the rescue. I don't see it as magnanimous move on their part, Adam. They are simply making a business pitch."

"Oh, I agree, but at the moment we're discussing potential benefits, not the drawbacks. Jenkins also pointed out we would be working under their legal umbrella."

"Meaning?"

"Meaning they would provide us free legal service, both personal and professional. And depending on the business arrangement, perhaps even corporate benefits, like retirement plans, something foreign to us."

"Adam, we may be gaining corporate benefits, but would we not be losing our corporate identity?"

"That's going to depend on the details of the proposed agreement. The question is how much independence we would be surrendering, starting with the case selection process. Who is going to have the final say on which ones we take on?"

"I do see one potential benefit in that regard," Tamra opined. "They could serve as a filter to the possible legal landmines of each case. There are always those we have to consider."

"True, but then there are other issues---potential conflicts of interest, the need to report to a supervisor, how it may affect the positive relationship we've developed with local law enforcement officials over the years---not to mention the more logistical items like office location. No question, there would be details galore to be worked out. Perhaps not so many if it was a retainer-type agreement, which could suffice, for all we know."

"Something along the lines of a rental car company operating in the maintenance section of a car dealership," Tamra suggested. "Have you consulted with your old boss on this?"

"Pete? No, though I definitely intend to before any final decision is made."

Adam was already having second thoughts on the proposed relationship, particularly its impact on the freedom of choice regarding the case selection guidelines. Currently, the procedure was greatly influenced by their location. They were operating out of a street-level office situated on the corner of a moderately busy street. Walk-in traffic was steady—granted, not always a good thing for a P.I. outfit. It led to a significant amount of "impulse buying," which was not in tune with most of the trade's target base. Passersby would spot the store sign and on the spur of the moment decide they would rid themselves of lingering suspicions that their spouses were cheating on them, or an employee of theirs had his or her hand in the till, or they wanted their outdoor cat trailed so they could find out where it was spending the day. Following one walk-in guy's request that they conduct a background check on his neighbor whom he suspected was a mass murderer, he joked to Tamra that they should post a sign on the front entrance stating *We don't do serial killers.* It was one of the reasons a growing number of private investigators were forsaking the brick-and-mortar store for the home office where there was less chance of the delusional individual wandering in off the street to seek their assistance. In a home-based operation it was much easier to concentrate on corporate clients who were interested in tackling problems like insurance fraud or employee theft. That's where the money was.

Yet, despite all the challenges posed by the walk-in trade, it did offer what Adam considered the most rewarding aspect of the profession---the opportunity to fix a family for the man or woman in the street. Tamra had picked up on this preference of his early on and had developed the skills to take on cases based on the attributes of clients, more so than the task involved, a distinction that greatly reduced the possibility of subsequent regret.

"In selecting clients, you want to pick someone whose side you wish to be on," he had advised her. "There are no honeymoon, probation, or engagement periods with clients. Therefore, you want to be on the same page with them from day one. Lawyers may look at it differently, giving greater consideration to the case."

Her earlier mention of a white knight potentially acting as a filter for the business brought him an inward smile, for there was no better filter than her in screening out the nightmare client.

"Maybe these two cases we're taking on simultaneously will give us an indication of how raising the production end of the operation impacts us...office-wise and field-wise," Tamra continued.

Adam glanced at the wall clock. "Maybe so...now, what was the second item you wanted to bring up before I head off?" he asked, hurrying her along.

"I received my first subpoena."

"Relating to Adam Fraley Private Investigations, I assume."

"Yes."

"Another good reason to join The Justice Brigade," he quipped. "Seriously, you are to be congratulated. I'm surprised it took this long. In this business you come to expect them. What does it pertain to?"

"Do you recall those background checks I conducted for the Midtown Mall security people for that job opening they had a few months back?"

"Sure do."

"One of the applicants is suing, claiming she lost out to a far less qualified candidate. I'm not sure why they want my testimony."

"Which side are you testifying for?"

"The security firm...any tips?"

"Stick to the facts of the background checks and be very careful with your opinions. I had a similar case not long after I first got into this business. I conducted background checks on a group of applicants for an upper level position in a banking firm. As in your case, one of the applicants sued for being bypassed for what she called a less qualified candidate. The bank felt they had a solid case and, in my opinion, they did. In the court testimony, however, one of the bank's personnel managers on the hiring panel stupidly commented on the witness stand that he considered the plaintiff a dullard. When the judge's final ruling came down in favor of the plaintiff, the word 'dullard' appeared five times in the written decision. He cited it as an example of a preconceived bias. As a result, the plaintiff ended up getting the job and the careless personnel manager wound up without one. He was fired."

"I'll be sure to watch my language," Tamra declared.

"When's the court date? It's not going to interfere with present business, is it?"

"No, it's a month away."

"You're fortunate, though I should say we're fortunate. Often those subpoenas are served hours in advance," he said. "Nothing like having a monkey wrench thrown into your regular workday plans before you even get started on them."

Adam paused a moment, reflecting on Tamra's proposal about who would handle which assignment. Both cases could present dangerous circumstances, he knew from previous experience, so trading cases based on the facts as presently known could be premature.

"Tamra, I'm not comfortable leaving you in charge of a domestic case that could go awry," he said.

"The future is always unclear, no matter what type of case we take on," she countered.

"This is the nature of the business we're in."

"Then promise me that you'll fill me in the moment your intuition tells you that you're in over your head."

"You'll be the first to know, she said, gathering her notes. "With that in mind, we best hit the road."

CHAPTER TWO

UNFAMILIAR AS ADAM WAS WITH THE NEIGHBORHOOD, IT TOOK him a while to find the rental house Manny Rivera reportedly resided in. As it turned out, it was located on a lot near the Coastal State College campus. The wood frame structure was definitely showing its age and lack of upkeep to the point of reaching eyesore status in comparison to the other well-kept, lower middle-class homes lining the block. Weeds were the property's dominant feature, having begun their steady climb up the sides of the house, after having strangled the life out of the lawn and nearly camouflaging completely a gravel driveway on which was parked an old Chevy Nova.

Adam pulled his pickup to a stop behind the Nova, hopped out and headed toward the front door. As he approached, he noticed a piece of paper flapping in the breeze that was attached to it. A closer look revealed it to be an eviction notice recently issued by the county.

He rapped hard on the door. Moments later, it swung halfway open. Standing there with one hand still clutching the knob was a short, shaggy-haired kid wearing cargo shorts, a brown t-shirt, battered sneakers, and a helluva worried look on his fresh face. "Yes," he said in a hesitant greeting.

"I'm looking for a fellow by the name of Manny Rivera. I've been informed he lives here."

"He's gone," the young man said hurriedly, as he started to close the door. "He no longer lives here."

"Gone where?" Adam asked with verve, placing his hand on the door with enough force to halt its movement.

"I'm not sure. Who wants to know?"

"I and a few other interested parties."

"Who are you?"

"Adam Fraley, private investigator. And you?"

"Timmy Stacy."

"I'd like to have a few minutes of your time, Timmy, to discuss a situation that has come up regarding Manny. May I come in?"

"I really have to run," Timmy said, making it sound more like a plea.

"It will only take a few minutes," Adam said in a conciliatory tone.

Reluctantly, Timmy opened the door, acquiescing to the request. Adam followed him into a living room that featured scattered pieces of furniture of frat house quality. Also featured was a sizable suitcase positioned by the front door. No doubt packed and ready to be grabbed, he surmised.

Adam settled into a badly frayed couch directly across from an equally frayed armchair Timmy had plopped into. "When did Manny leave?" he asked his host.

"About two months ago. Why do you ask? Is he in some kind of trouble?"

"I was about to ask you that same question. His parents seem to think he is."

Timmy rubbed his hands while glancing at his suitcase. "Is it call-the-cops kind of trouble they are thinking he is in?"

"You tell me," Adam said, in as commanding a tone as he could muster without breaking the line of communication between the two.

Timmy continued with his hand rubbing, offering no response.

"When did you last speak with him?" Adam asked, nudging him along.

"This morning, on the phone."

"Where is he?"

"Las Vegas."

"What's he doing there?"

Again, Timmy lapsed into a silence, obviously waging an internal debate as to how far he should tag along with the questioning.

"Look, you asked if it was a call-the-cops situation," Adam prodded. "Well, the longer it takes for me to find him, the closer it comes to calling it that, which is why it is important for you to tell me whatever you know about his current whereabouts and what he's up to. So, what's he doing in Las Vegas?" Adam repeated, giving him another verbal poke.

This time Timmy abruptly shifted in his chair and clasped his hands in his lap. "Okay, I'll tell you what I know."

Adam nodded his approval.

"Manny is from Colombia, South America. His parents sent him here to attend school at Coastal State College. I met him on campus during registration. We were signing up for many of the same classes. After completing registration, he wanted to know if I would like to share a rental house he already had moved into. I told him I wasn't sure if I could afford off-campus housing, but he offered to give me a good deal, so I took him up on the offer. It wasn't long after classes had started, I realized Manny was far less interested in getting an education than he was in partying. He began skipping classes and inviting girls over for late-night stays. Needless to say, it wasn't the ideal atmosphere for studying. What made things worse were his frequent weekend trips to Vegas where he picked up a bad gambling habit."

Timmy was now speaking with the hyper energy and unease of someone who was thinking he was a step away from big trouble.

"He's under twenty-one I take it," Adam interjected.

"Yes, and that's what led him into dangerous territory. In order to wager, he sought out an underground sports gambling operation..."

"Illegal, you're saying."

"Yes. Manny would often tell me how surprised I would be at how many things related to gambling were illegal in Las Vegas. Anyway, he began pouring money into bets and apparently came up on the losing end of most of them, piling up a big debt."

"Where was he getting the money to wager?"

"From his parents, who are very wealthy. Apparently, they are completely unaware he has been throwing away the allowance they've been sending him to feed his gambling habit."

"Must be a nice allowance," Adam commented.

"They intended it for living and educational expenses, though little of the funds went to either."

"There was no system to account for his spending?"

"Not really. They simply deposited funds into a bank account he had set up...no questions asked. Manny would often request increases in his allowance, claiming he had to add additional classes or some such thing."

"Did you ever speak with the parents?"

"On occasion they would call when he was not here. I frequently would have to lie about his whereabouts, which I now regret. Sometimes they would ask how he was doing in his classes, which led to more lying on my part. Unfortunately, I found out just how easy it was to lie on his behalf when you're living here rent free on his dime."

"Have you talked with them recently?"

"It's been a while since I've spoken to them."

"Have you been in regular contact with Manny during his absence?"

"No. I had not heard from him until the other day. He called in a frenzy asking me to wire him bus money to get home. He had completely blown all his funds and had no way to get back. I told him I would, and I did. This morning he called again and he was even more stressed out than he was before I sent the money. He said the gambling syndicate he was dealing with was out to get him for the unpaid debt he had piled up."

"How much debt?"

"Fifty thousand bucks."

"Fifty thousand?" Adam softly whistled his astonishment. "For a kid!"

"Like I said, his parents were free with the funds."

"Sounds like they weren't free enough to free him from his debt," Adam said. "How was the syndicate out to get him?"

"From the way he talked, I took it to mean they were threatening physical harm of some sort. What really had him bothered was he spotted one of their so-called enforcers tailing him."

"This morning?"

"Yes."

"Did he describe him?"

"No...said he recognized him as one of their enforcers. He referred to him as their muscle guy, which might give you a clue to his size."

"Does he know the guy's name?"

"No, just kept referring to him as 'the mob guy.'"

"Where was he calling from?"

"The Vegas bus station where he was about to board. He said he was heading to Tampa via Kansas City."

"Why Kansas City? If I recall my geography correctly, it's not exactly on a straight-line path from there to here."

"I asked him the same thing. He said there was a big convention breaking up and many of the buses heading out of town were filled up and he didn't want to wait."

"What time was this?"

"An hour or so ago."

Adam checked his watch. "Meaning it would have been around eight o'clock in Vegas."

"That's about right. Before I could ask him anything else, he said he had to go and hung up."

"Rule number one in Vegas---always pay your gambling debts,"

Adam said. "The old saw, 'What happens in Vegas stays in Vegas,' does not apply to gambling debts. They are not forgotten nor forgiven, no matter the distances or boundaries."

Timmy nodded, as though he was learning fast the ramifications of the topic at hand.

"You have a photo of Manny I could have?"

"There should be one laying around here somewhere," he said, jumping up from his chair and disappearing into a back room. Moments later he was back with two photographs in hand. One depicted Manny and two older individuals, apparently shot a few years ago in his home country. The other was of Timmy and Manny taken in front of the rental house before its weed-infestation days. But for the somewhat darker-skinned Manny, the roommates were much alike in their general physical appearance---short and lithe with engaging smiles spread across their boyish faces. "A carefree guy, you would say?" Adam asked, gazing at the photo.

"Carefree and careless," Timmy replied.

"There have been careless instances other than this one?"

"Oh, yeah. He was always coming up with these get-rich-quick schemes. Why, I don't know. He was already rich with his parents' money."

"Maybe he has an entrepreneurial bent to him," Adam half-jested.

Timmy shrugged, as if he hadn't given his roommate's motivation much thought. "One time he set up a personal message delivery service. He operated it right out of this house."

"What sort of messages?"

"Messages that people find difficult to deliver in person...like a girlfriend telling a boyfriend she is no longer interested in seeing him, or a message from a secret admirer to the object of his or her affection, or even those from small business owners to employees telling them they had been terminated. They ran the gamut."

"Sounds to me like a business begging for a risk manager."

"Manny was always saying the key to the business was to get in and get out fast when delivering the message. One time he didn't get out fast enough and took a fist to the face from a jealous boyfriend who didn't appreciate the getting-dumped note he was handed. It was enough for him to give it all up."

Adam glanced at his watch. "Well, I have to be running along. You got a phone number where you can be reached, in case I need to touch base with you?"

Timmy again disappeared into a back room and came out with a slip of paper on which he had scribbled down a phone number.

"This is the number here?" Adam asked.

"No, it's my parents' number. That's where I'll be staying. They live in Sarasota. The number here has been cut off by the phone company for lack of payment. The call I received this morning was the last one."

"So, you have no idea whether Manny actually got on that bus."

"No, but I don't think he really had much choice from the way he talked. He had a ticket to get him out of town and nothing else."

"Let's hope the guy tailing him didn't take the same stage out of town," Adam said, ending his visit.

―――――

FOLLOWING HIS MEETING WITH TIMMY, Adam hustled back to the office to ponder his next move.

"That was quick," Tamra said in greeting him. "Case closed?"

"It may be for us."

He briefed her on his visit and his indecision on whether to end their involvement. "He's been found. Anything else is beyond our purview...right?"

"Has he been found? Sounds to me like you're trying to convince yourself of it," Tamra responded from across the room. "Finding is seeing him in person, Adam. Can't you at least call the cops...let them know the kid's plight?"

"Call which cops in which jurisdiction? And what chance is there of any law enforcement unit launching an investigation based on virtually no hard evidence, just the hearsay of a college kid?"

"Maybe Timmy or Manny will call them."

"Two scared college kids...no way."

"The gambling syndicate...maybe they'll call."

Adam hurled a puzzled look his colleague's way. "The illegal gambling outfit calling the cops? You serious?"

"No, but you seem determined to pass the baton to someone," she countered. "You're just not sure to whom. The point is I've never known you to give up on a case."

Adam leaned back in his chair and reflected a moment. "When's your client scheduled to be here?" he asked in resignation to the course correction he was about to make.

Tamra glanced at the wall clock. "In about an hour."

Adam at once opened one of his desk drawers to retrieve a road atlas and a phone book from which he located an eight hundred number for Transcontinental Bus Lines. "Might as well start with the biggest," he said to himself, referring to the outfit that nearly monopolized the cross-country bus business. A customer relations rep was soon on the line addressing his question of whether there were any buses leaving Las Vegas for Kansas City this morning. "There was only one," she informed him. "It left at 8:00 a.m."

Though he knew what the answer was to his next question, he asked anyway. "Can you tell me if a particular individual was on that bus?" He was right of course.

"No sir, we are not allowed to divulge that information. If it's an emergency, I would suggest contacting your nearest law enforcement agency." He was about to end his questioning, when one more popped into his head. "Can you tell me two or three major stops the bus makes along the way to KC and how long the entire trip takes?"

A brief silence ensued before she was back on the line. "Albuquerque, Oklahoma City, Wichita, and Emporia are four stops. The entire route to KC takes twenty-two hours."

Adam next checked the road atlas and the general path the bus would take. Wichita, the last sizable city on the route, was about two hundred miles from KC. That meant it would be reached in about eighteen or nineteen hours---three or four in the morning. He could fly to KC but chances were Manny would be changing buses there to travel on to Tampa. No, he wanted to intercept the bus at an earlier stop to give him a better idea of the people and logistics involved. If there was a muscle man on board, KC would be a good place for him to make whatever manner of move he was going to make on Manny and still be able to disappear into the crowd. Manny wouldn't dare get off the bus before KC, Adam surmised, or he'd risk a confrontation with the mob guy. The kid's best option was to stick with his plan and hope he could make the transfer to the bus headed for Tampa while still in the public eye. Quickly, Adam was back on the phone to Transcontinental, booking a ride from Wichita to KC. The bus was scheduled to depart Wichita tomorrow at 4:00 a.m. To complete his itinerary, he checked with the airlines and booked an afternoon flight to Wichita arriving at 7:00 p.m. this evening.

With his bookings complete, he turned to see Tamra gazing at him from across the room with a soft smile on her face.

"What?" he asked.

"My road warrior," she responded, with a cheery smile on her face.

CHAPTER THREE

MICKEY RILEY WAS A COLLEGE PHYSICAL EDUCATION INSTRUCTOR who fit the description of one—medium height, muscular build, buzz haircut, clear facial features, intense brown eyes, and a voice that would fill a gymnasium with little effort. The clothing he wore no doubt was similar to what he donned for his classes, Tamra reckoned—form-fitting tan t-shirt, khaki shorts, and dark brown walking boots.

"So, Mr. Riley, your sister and brother-in-law have gone missing and you believe she is being held against her will by him. Is that correct?" she politely asked from across her desk.

"Yes, ma'am."

"What makes you think this?"

"Mainly from feedback I've received from my other sister, Meg, who lives here and has attempted without much success to keep in touch with her."

"You don't live in Tampa?"

"No, I live about fifty miles north of here."

"Is Meg an older or younger sister?"

"She's the oldest of the siblings."

"Your other sister—the one missing. Her name is Susan, right?"

"Right."

"How often have you been checking on her?"

"Very often, up until the time they disappeared. When I did call to speak with Susan, her husband invariably would say she was busy without saying at what. When I asked him to have her call me, he said he would, though she never did."

"Do you believe your messages were passed along?"

"No, not at all."

"How did you come to the conclusion he has in effect imprisoned her?"

"Like I said, my sister, Meg, has been trying like hell to touch base with her, but every attempt to do so has been rebuffed by this jerk. We are a very close family. Are you familiar with the old line, 'Lord help the mister who comes between me and my sister'?"

Tamra nodded.

"Well, that pretty much sums up Meg's attitude at the moment. She's even gone over to his place unannounced and knocked on the door in an attempt to see her, all to no avail. He was always prepared with a reason to deny her request, including the obviously fake one that her sister did not want to see her."

"How long have they been married?"

Riley thought a moment. "Six or seven years."

"No children?"

"Thankfully, no."

"Is there physical abuse toward her?"

"Meg believes it's mostly mental, though there's no way to be certain without seeing her."

"What's his business?"

"He's a lawyer."

"Why do you suppose he picked up and left with her?"

"Probably because he was tired of the pestering he was getting from Meg and me."

"Why not divorce her? It's not like he's dependent on her, emotionally or financially, from what you tell me."

"Meg is convinced she helps project a false front for him, like a flower shop does for mobsters trying to hide their activities."

"How so?"

"He represents a lot of big-time crooks involved in gambling, prostitution, witness tampering, and so on. Apparently, a lot of the grime from working with them has rubbed off on him. Susan represents normalcy—the clean-cut family image he continues to try and portray to the public. How could a wonderful wife like her be associated with anything crooked? That's her primary contribution to the marriage in his eyes, we believe."

"What exactly do you expect of me?" Tamra asked. "I will tell you up front that I will not be party to any violence. I'm sure you are aware domestic disturbances can escalate quickly."

"All I want is for you to find them. I will then go and get her. I have no intention of engaging in a physical altercation with this guy, nor do I expect you or anyone else to do so."

"Okay, for us to get started I will need photos of your sister and her husband, preferably current ones."

"I brought them along," Riley said, opening up a folder he had in hand containing two large photos. "This one is of my sister Susan," he said, handing over one of them. "Her married name is Carson...Susan Carson."

Tamra studied the photo for a moment, noting the definite facial resemblance to her brother before setting it aside.

Riley handed her the second photo. "This one is of her husband...Wade Carson."

Tamra took it in hand, pondering the image, then slowly placed it next to the one of Riley's sister. "Where is their former home?" she asked.

"In the Ybor City vicinity."

"How long has it been since they lived there?"

Riley shrugged. "Several months. There are a couple of guys living there now but they claim to have no idea where my sister or her husband presently live."

"Do you have any idea?"

"Meg says that during the early years of their marriage, they spent quite a bit of time visiting Gasparilla Island south of here. Are you familiar with that area?"

"Yes, I've also made some day trips down there. Nice place. Does Meg know where they stayed on the island?"

"No, otherwise both of us would have hustled down there and beat on their door."

"One last question...do you know what model of vehicle Mr. Carson drives?"

"Yes, a late-model, powder blue Lexus. And before you ask, I don't know the license plate number."

"Okay, Mr. Riley, this should give me enough to start on," Tamra said, rising from her chair to exchange a handshake with him. "I will get back in touch with you as soon as I come up with something definite as to their whereabouts. Meantime, let me know of any new developments on your end."

Not long after Riley left the office, Tamra resumed her contemplation of the Wade Carson photo, waging an internal debate over whether to withdraw herself from the case. The words she had spoken to Adam when he was considering dropping his came to mind. "I have never known you to give up on a case," she had said to him with conviction. The same, no doubt, would be repeated by him to her in this instance, if he were here. And like Adam, she wasted no time in dismissing the thought of quitting. Still, the image in the photograph lingered with her late into the evening, conjuring up other images, ones that could have been lifted from an album of her life, if such a record existed. In the end, it took a late-night call from Adam to break the spell.

"I'm sitting here in a top-floor room of a Wichita Holiday Inn, looking out over the downtown area, as the sun sets behind it."

"What's there to see?"

"Picture a four-square-block section of downtown Tampa with a slow-moving river flowing through it. Not far off is a large, single-level, circular building that I assume is a convention center or exhibition hall of some sort. Across from it is a good-sized public library building."

"You left out the bus station."

"I can't pick it out from here. The front desk clerk assures me it's eight blocks away."

"The kind of early morning walk you enjoy taking."

"Not three-in-the-morning early and not when you're lugging an overnight bag with you," Adam pointed out. "How about you? Any chance your case will be taking you to parts unknown?"

"Gasparilla Island for sure."

"Well, you're certainly familiar with the area...one of your favorite old hangouts, you keep telling me. Sounds like a vacation, not an assignment. Do you want to give me the details?"

"I'll save them for you when you get back," she said, feeling there was no pressing need to bring them to his attention now, even though she had promised to notify him of any gut instincts to the contrary. Besides, under the new setup, she had complete decision-making power for any case she was working,

"Two for the road...that's us, Tamra," he said, as if proposing a toast.

"Two for the road, Adam," she said in return, her mind at the moment more attuned to the road of life and whether it was taking her on a dangerous detour.

CHAPTER FOUR

ADAM WAS A HALF HOUR EARLY TO THE STATION. Unfortunately, the bus was running an hour late, according to the ticket agent, an elderly gent who looked like he was suffering from a chronic case of sleep deprivation. No doubt an occupational hazard caused by too much waiting for late-arriving buses in early-morning hours, he mused. "An accident south of here slowed them plenty," the old man drawled.

He took a seat in the waiting room, empty but for him. Soon, he was dozing off, the drone of a nearby vending machine having lulled him into a stupor until the beep of a horn, signaling the arrival of the bus, brought him and the station to life. Surprisingly, he was the lone passenger waiting to board in contrast to the dozen who were exiting, none of whom, he carefully noted, came close to fitting the description of Manny. Half of those disembarking were doing so for a break. The others had reached their destination. Once the driver had retrieved the luggage for those who had stored it in the carriage bin and everyone else had returned from their breaks, the station agent notified Adam he was free to board.

"Showtime," he murmured to himself as he hopped up the entrance steps and handed his ticket to the driver. "There should be some empty seats toward the back," he was advised. Easing his way down the main aisle, he carefully eyed the lineup of passengers. The interior was dark but there was enough ambient light emanating from the lighted driver's perch and station to allow him a gander at each rider. All were in various states of sleep and postures from the fetal to the side-sleeper. Five rows down he came to a near stop. There, in a reclining position, was Manny, his head propped against the window, his satchel in his lap. For an instant he considered taking the empty seat beside him. However, he decided he would first observe from a distance until he'd gained a better sense of all his options. Continuing on, he found a vacant row toward the back and settled in. Moments later the driver ignited the engine and they were off to the interstate. In no time he drifted into a light sleep, confident that for the time being Manny was going nowhere, as long as the bus was on the move.

———

ADAM WOKE WITH A START. For a split second, he had to reintroduce himself to his environs. The sun had risen, its morning rays streaming through the windows, flooding the interior with bright light. Most of the passengers were indulging in their favorite time-killing pastimes, from reading to gawking out the window— all but one, that is. Manny Rivera was missing. *How the hell?* They couldn't be more than a half hour out of Wichita. Surely, the bus had not made an unexpected stop during his nap or else he would have been awakened by a sudden slowing of the vehicle, a honk of the horn, a hiss of the brakes, or the clamor of the door opening. Then it hit him, the guy who had yet to clear the morning cobwebs from his head. This was a bus with a restroom at the back end of it. No sooner had it dawned on him than the door to it swung open and out stepped Manny to retake his seat up front. Once the kid had settled in, Adam took a closer look at the lineup of passengers. Abandoning his seat, he casually strolled to the front of the bus to ask the driver, a husky fellow with a friendly face, how far they were from the next stop.

"Emporia is our next stop—about an hour and a half away. Here's a route map you can have," he said, slipping one out from a folder propped against his seat and handing it to him.

Adam turned to begin a slow procession back down the aisle, eyeing each passenger row by row along the way. Among them were a young mother and her toddler son, an elderly lady busy knitting, a Hispanic couple engaged in a spirited discussion, followed by Manny, who at the moment was staring out the window with a forlorn look on his face. In the row directly behind him was a man dressed in a dark pinstripe suit with a vest, white shirt, loosened black tie, and a copy of the Las Vegas Sun resting in his lap, He was followed by a college-age girl with her head buried in a textbook, a bohemian-looking fellow sitting in the row across from her, a vagabond-appearing gent with stacks of "stuff" in the seat beside him, two more college-age kids, a scruffy, rusty-haired guy with a hand-held accordion positioned by his side, and a pony-tailed fellow with a taut, tanned face and a backpack stashed beside him who looked as though he was headed home from a long trek through the mountains. Lastly, he noted a geyser in farmer's overalls who sat watching Foghorn Leghorn cartoons on a portable TV he had brought along.

Adam took his seat in the row behind the farmer and pondered Manny's plight. The kid was $50,000 in arrears to an underground gambling operation, an obligation they were not about to let him walk away from. The debt collector was likely on board and from all indications was sitting in the row directly behind his target. Who else would wear an outfit like he was sporting on a cross-county bus trip? Sometimes the stereotypes fit. The man got on in Vegas, wore the traditional garb of a mob guy, and was glaring at the back of Manny's head as though he was going to wrap a ligature around his neck as soon as the circumstances allowed it. Obviously, Manny sensed it with his numerous over-the-shoulder glances to see if his tormentor was still tailgating him.

The question of why the gambling syndicate had allowed Manny to run up that big of a debt popped into Adam's head. Perhaps he made good on his previous payments, running up a credit score sufficient for a friendly dealer to allow him to go all in on a big wager. Certainly, it was reasonable for Manny to think he could turn to his parents for help in case he dug himself a hole, just as it was reasonable for his frustrated parents to refuse to cover the debt and instead enlist Adam Fraley Private Investigations for help in tracking him down. That they were aware of his debt, however, was never made known to Tamra.

So why not go up and introduce yourself to Manny? Tell him you're here to escort him back to Tampa. Sure, and risk a confrontation on the bus?

How many times in the past during the course of an investigation did he have to remind himself he was not a law enforcement officer? No, he would wait until the end of the line in Kansas City where the situation would come to a head. Then he would make his move when all three players had no choice but to depart the bus, a circumstance Manny's pursuer no doubt looked favorably upon for a move of his own.

The guffaws of the farmer in the row ahead of him every time Foghorn Leghorn would spank the dog that was tormenting him without letup brought Adam's attention back to the other passengers and the social milieu developing on board, not all of which was cordial. The bohemian guy across the aisle from the college girl had been hitting on her all morning. By now it was bordering on harassment to the degree she had shifted from her row's aisle seat to the window seat to distance herself from him. It did little good. The guy's advances were becoming blatant enough for everyone around them to see, so much so the mob guy, as Adam now identified him, turned his attention from the back of Manny's head to the scene playing out behind him. He, however, was not one to let matters stand. Instead, he rose from his seat and stepped back to where the persistent suitor was still leaning halfway across the aisle. "Listen, you Putz, are you too damn dense to see this girl has more interest in the book she's reading than you?" he growled in words heated enough to scald a tongue. "One more word out of you and I'm going to turn that ugly kisser of yours into a much uglier one." Stunned by the dictum, the harasser slithered his torso back into his window seat, at which point the mob guy slowly turned to head back to his seat.

A gentleman gangster, Adam mused. *Score one for the underworld.*

"Hey, settle down back there," the bus driver shouted out, following the outburst.

Adam recognized the display of chauvinism as an act much in keeping with the mob's code of conduct, a traditional behavior handed down from one family don to the other. In no way did it negate the reality that there was a hit man operating behind the public facade. There were three traditional commandments the mob guy must adhere to. The first—do nothing that can be considered disloyal to the organization. The second—don't ever steal money belonging to members of it. The third—follow orders. Violations of any one of these commandments carried a stiff penalty, mitigating circumstances be damned. If violators were of adult age, they were subject to severe punishments. The word "mercy" was not part of the mob's vocabulary. Every mob member learned this from day one.

A nervous quiet had settled over the coach. From the looks on the passengers' faces, Adam sensed the universal feeling among them was that this ride could not end fast enough. One incident was enough. In the meantime, he expected a lot of tiptoeing up and down the aisles.

Figuring order had been restored at least for the moment, Adam immersed himself in the view of the passing countryside. This was as close to a cross-county trip he had taken since his great train expedition at age twenty-two that took him from Tampa to Seattle with stops in Philadelphia and Chicago along the way. He loved train travel as opposed to bus trips—less confining---more opportunities to get out of your seat and roam to club, dome, and dining cars. And if you weren't operating on a tight budget, you could splurge for a cabin for optimum privacy. At his young age, however, he was still traveling the frugal path and riding coach. Nevertheless, it turned out to be a memorable trip, made more so by a stroke of luck occurring three quarters of the way into his journey in of all places Cody, Wyoming, the eastern gateway to

Yellowstone National Park. Approaching the town's tiny train station, he noticed through his coach window a small group of travelers gathered on the depot's platform who were waiting to board. Among them was a strikingly attractive young woman with long, light-brown hair wearing a suede jacket, powder blue jeans, and a pleasant countenance. The seat next to him was vacant. What were the odds, he thought, of her holding a ticket with that seat number? Whatever the odds...short or long, he came out a winner. The seat belonged to her.

The last leg of the trip, from Cody to Seattle, was the stuff of dreams for Adam. The two hit it off immediately. Aubrey was her name...a recent college graduate who was headed to Seattle to visit some friends before starting a new job as a financial analyst for a firm in San Diego. They were two strangers placed side by side by benevolent fate on a long-distance train. In the course of minutes, they were strangers no more and as comfortable as could be in conversation with each other. The getting-to-know-you continued over supper in the dining car. After the meal came the highlight of the trip when the two decided to head up to the dome car to spend the evening watching the majestic western landscape drift by. Their reverie continued into the late night and early morning hours, at which point they had the dome car all to themselves. It had become their own private theater with a sky-wide screen displaying a canvas of moonlight-bathed mountains haloed by soft starlight. In the midst of the show, Aubrey rested her head on his shoulder and fell asleep. Adam didn't sleep a wink.

The first streaks of dawn returned them to reality. Their time together was about to come to an end. They returned to their coach where passengers were gathering their belongings in preparation for their arrival at the station.

"How long are you planning to stay in Seattle?" she asked.

"I'm not sure. I was thinking of extending my trip by catching the Alaskan ferry and traveling the inland route up to Juneau and back."

"How long does it take?" she asked.

"About a week...have you seen Alaska?"

"No, but I've got it on my wish list."

"Want to tag along?" he asked straightforwardly.

"I just might do that," she said. "My friends will be waiting at the Seattle station for me. As a courtesy I should discuss it with them first. Perhaps they'll be willing to wait another week for whatever they had planned."

It proved too good to be true. When they disembarked the train in Seattle, her friends were waiting for her a short distance down the platform.

"I'll be right back," she said and loped down to meet them.

Adam watched with great anticipation as she spoke with her friends, all of them appearing around her age. Every few seconds their heads turned from their huddle to glimpse him as she proposed the idea of spending a week in Alaska.

In a trice she broke from them and jogged back to where Adam was waiting patiently.

"I'm sorry, Adam, but I'll have to decline your invitation. It was my friends, after all, I came to Seattle to see and to alter plans at this stage would be more than rude of me, I'm afraid."

"I understand," he said, knowing full well if he were one of her friends, he too would be discouraging her from taking off for Alaska with a stranger.

Aubrey retrieved a pen and slip of paper from her purse and jotted down her phone number. "I hope to hear from you," she said before heading off with her friends.

He tossed away the idea of adding an Alaskan leg to the trip, the fervor for it having been drained out of him by her decision. Instead, he booked a room in a nearby waterfront hotel and spent the week dining on salmon sandwiches and huckleberry ice cream while watching the ferry boats go in and out of the port, occasionally hopping one himself for a leisurely ride across Puget Sound.

Once he had returned home to Tampa, he debated long and hard whether to call Aubrey, wary of starting up a long-distance relationship and all of the challenges it presented. In the end his procrastination cost him. When he finally did call, her number was out of commission, indicating she was now on her new job and no longer in Cody. He would have let it rest, if not for his entry into the private investigation business two years later. Learning the art of finding missing persons instilled in him enough incentive to consider tracking down the gal who continued to linger in the recesses of his mind. That was until Tamra Fugit entered his life, which eventually erased any interest or memories of former flames.

———

"I SAY, son...quit that daydreaming of yours!"

Foghorn Leghorn's admonition, albeit from a TV screen, catapulted Adam from the past to the present, from visions of soaring mountains to the sight of a vast plain he was visioning through the bus window. A roadside sign immediately came into view. "Matfield Green rest stop one mile ahead," it read. "Matfield Green...Matfield Green," he repeated to himself, triggering a memory from long ago. He was sure it must be the same Matfield Green a favorite uncle of his was referring to when telling him the story of a tragedy that captured the nation's attention back in the early 1930s.

"A short distance away, maybe eight miles or so, from this tiny town of Matfield Green in Kansas was the spot where the University of Notre Dame's legendary football coach, Knute Rockne, was killed in a plane crash while traveling cross country to Los Angeles," he had related. According to his uncle, by the time the government investigators arrived on the scene, everything but the engine, wings, and propeller was taken by souvenir hunters.

Rockne's status with the public was on par with presidents and caused a massive outpouring of grief, especially among football fans like his uncle. In the end, the cause of the crash was never officially determined, despite all the attention given it.

You never know when a bit of history will come passing by, Adam mused, *or in this instance fall out of the sky in an isolated open field not far from where a routine rest stop would one day sit.*

Once past Matfield Green, another sign caught Adam's

attention, advising passing motorists they were entering the Flint Hills. The plains of Kansas and hills were two geographical features he never associated with each other. Curious as to the hills' existence, he snatched the pamphlet from his shirt pocket that the driver had given him and casually perused it. Sure enough, an insert to the road map succinctly addressed the topic. The Flint Hills were the spawning grounds for the tall grass prairie, a giant expanse of land reaching from Canada to Texas and Kansas to Indiana. The sea of grass was at one time a shallow sea of water, transformed over the years by the agricultural industry.

Adam set aside the pamphlet to peer out the window at the passing scene. Rolling hills, sloping gently uphill and downhill and carpeted by large swaths of tall grass stretched to the far horizon. The grasses were bending in waves to the breezes, while shadows formed from drifting cotton ball clouds intermittently darkened portions of the fields. The grasses may not be as high as an elephant's eye, but were at least as tall as a buffalo's, he observed. The vision brought to mind Tamra's often stated favorite thing to do in life---take long walks in wide open spaces. She couldn't ask for a better place than here, he reckoned.

———

"By God, that's the biggest one of those I've seen in a long time," the farmer said aloud, directing his comment to the guy sitting behind him.

"What is...you mean that silo out there?" Adam asked.

The farmer shut off his TV, lowered the back of his aisle seat enough to open a crack between seats to chat with Adam ensconced in his window seat. "That's not a silo my friend. That's a grain elevator. I call them the castles of the plains."

"What's the difference?" Adam asked, gazing indifferently out the window.

"They differ in their design. Grain bins are shorter and much fatter. They're used for the dry storage of grain—wheat, corn, soybeans and the like. Silos store silage—chopped corn, grasses, and so on. Normally, they're taller and skinnier than grain elevators. That one we're looking at has to be close to a hundred and fifty feet high. I've been to the top of them. The view from up there is better than any view you get from the top of a twenty-five-story building. Sitting out there all by its lonesome don't give you the right perspective of just how big a structure it is," he drawled. "If there was a barn standing next to it, you'd think it was a dog house."

"What you're saying is that it's tall enough for a worker to be wary of accidentally falling off of it," Adam said, watching the building slowly disappear from view, leaving the flat lands unobstructed to the eye once again.

"Not only falling off it, but more to the point, falling into it," the farmer continued.

"You're telling me the grain, if there is grain in it, wouldn't cushion your fall?"

"Cushion you? Hell, it will swallow you up. Workers who accidentally fall into the stuff can end up dead. It's like stepping into quicksand. The pressure from the grain on the body makes it difficult to breathe. To make matters worse, rescuing workers in those conditions is a logistical nightmare."

"What are they doing inside it to get themselves in that predicament in the first place?" Adam asked. "The odor alone is enough to choke you to death, if it's anything like what I've inhaled on the few occasions I've been around grain elevators."

"Sometimes the grain in the bins becomes caked, requiring workers to walk it down..."

"Meaning what?" Adam interjected.

"Meaning they walk on top of it to smooth the flow from the chute at the bottom of the elevator."

"So, the corpses can go with the flow," Adam cracked in a strained attempt at humor.

"Hey, buddy—don't think it can't happen. Years ago, there was a dangerous convict who escaped on foot from the Kansas State Penitentiary at Lansing—not far from here, by the way. State troopers combed every foot of these parts trying to find him but with no luck. Several months later some workers in Kansas City were unloading a rail car full of grain and noticed some human remains mixed in with the load. It turned out to be the remains of the escaped convict. Investigators concluded the guy went hiding in a grain bin and somehow ended up getting sucked into the pile. The medical examiner determined he suffocated to death." The farmer reached between the seats and patted Adam on the knee. "I often wondered what would have happened if his remains had gone undiscovered. Hell, he could have ended up as part of some family's casserole. Ever hear of such a thing?" asked the storyteller with a big chuckle.

"No, but I've read of such a thing," Adam answered, dissipating the mirthful look on his fellow traveler's face.

"Oh yeah...where?"

"In a Shakespeare play...Titus Andronicus."

"You read Shakespeare on a bus?"

"Mostly in a classroom and on a train while commuting back and forth to college."

"The same thing happened in this play of his?"

"Similar to it. A Roman general kills two men who had assaulted his daughter, leaving her in terrible shape. He then grinds the killers' bodies into a powder which he cooks into a pie and serves to their mother."

"She eats it?"

"Sure does. To top it off, he kills the mother too, as a kind of just desserts."

"Say, that's some vengeful thinking on the part of old Willie. He thinks the way I do when I'm in a foul mood," the farmer chuckled. "Anyway, as I said, those grain elevators can be a death trap."

"I'll keep that in mind the next time I go looking for a missing person," Adam said in a disinterested manner, signaling his desire to close the conversation.

The farmer readjusted his seat and went back to watching his cartoons.

Adam resumed his contemplation of the passing countryside.

From grain elevators to Shakespeare and back again to Foghorn Leghorn. It was enough to give a mind whiplash, he figured.

———

A SIGNPOST ANNOUNCED that Emporia was five miles up the road. In due time hints of a city ahead sporadically came into view---scattered whitewashed homes, followed by storage facilities of various shapes and sizes, a random fast food restaurant, a truck stop, and a trailer park. Exiting the interstate, the bus turned onto an industrial road that eventually led them to a small, bare concrete building which served as the depot.

"Emporia...fifteen-minute stop," the driver called out.

All Adam knew of Emporia was that it was a college town and, if he recalled right, home to a famous little newspaper---the Emporia Gazette. Famous for what, he wasn't sure.

Several of the college kids got off, replaced by other students boarding for the remainder of the trip to Kansas City. Two adults disembarked---the cartoon-loving farmer, and the knitting lady who, before she departed, shuffled over to the homeless-looking man and handed him a dollar bill. The guy held it up to the light to examine it carefully, as if it might be counterfeit, before shoving it into his pocket.

"Kansas City, here we come!" the driver announced, bounding back up the steps to his perch.

"How far behind schedule are we?" the pony-tailed passenger shouted out.

"Forty-five minutes," the driver responded.

"Any chance of making some of it up?" came the follow-up.

"On a normal day, yes, but I'm told we may be running into some rough weather along the way, which may slow us up."

"A storm along the way and a good chance of a bigger one at the end," Adam murmured to himself.

CHAPTER FIVE

THE ROAD TO BOCA GRANDE WAS A PICTURESQUE ONE THAT Tamra always looked forward to seeing. From the causeway tollbooth to the town, the route over Gasparilla Island cut through a gallery of Florida greenery, featuring a wealth of finely manicured native tropical plants. The view was enough to take her mind off Mr. and Mrs. Carson, at least until she came upon the little pink library on the edge of town. It was here she began her quest.

Prior to her departure, she had conducted a basic computer search to determine whether there were public records linking Susan or Wade Carson to the island. The result was none which came as no great surprise to her, considering their taking up residency here was too recent an event, if in fact they resided here at all. As a result, she shifted her focus at the library to local, miscellaneous resources of a current nature, browsing through bulletins, newsletters, announcements, and the like for any mention of their names. Again, she came up empty. "Enough with the written records," she thought. Boca Grande was a tiny town and stood as the centerpiece of the island. Both residents and tourists, whether coming or going, made a point of stopping there for supplies, directions, or simply to soak in the atmosphere of a way of life fading fast from the Florida landscape. Within this provincial world casual conversation flowed freely between visitors and town folk. It wasn't the proverbial "everyone knows everyone" environment of small-town America, but it was the next best thing to tap into, she decided.

Back on the road, she headed for the town's old-time general store where she leisurely perused the crowded shelves and strolled the narrow aisles, casually striking up conversations with the customers and staff. Whenever the opportunity arose, she would innocently pose the question, "By chance, do you know of a Susan or Wade Carson who reside here?" Initially, she shunned showing photos, her past experiences having taught her they often raised suspicions regarding her motives for wanting to locate a person. If local residents displayed any spark of recognition, then, yes, she would dig them out for a look-see. All of her probing, however, was getting her nowhere, so she ended the effort. Before leaving she purchased some food items to take with her to a cozy motel she had stayed in on previous visits. She was quickly adapting to the laid-back style of the town, exemplified by the numerous golf carts sharing the road with her, a commonplace mode of transportation on the island.

Once settled in her room, Tamra took to planning the remainder of her day. On her to-do list were visits to the local historical society, chamber of commerce, and island tourist information center to continue her name-dropping. Given time she would even make a point of walking the streets, all the while keeping an eye out for a blue Lexus.

She saved for the last stop of the day the vintage railway station that had been transformed into an indoor-outdoor restaurant and the little ice cream shop right around the corner from it. Donning a yellow sundress and a pair of her favorite walking shoes, she stepped out of her room into the bright noonday sun. At once, she realized she had forgotten to bring along a hat. No problem. She'd rely on Boca Grande's abundance of banyan trees lining the streets for shade.

FIVE HOURS LATER, following an afternoon of meeting, greeting, listening, and probing the citizenry, she was sitting at the railway station restaurant, munching on a grouper sandwich, having scored a zero for the day. Oh, she'd learned plenty more about the island, particularly how its early development was tied closely to the burgeoning phosphate business in Central Florida. For distribution purposes, a sea lane was later developed to transport the mineral to overseas customers. Gasparilla was chosen as the site for a port and before long trucks were hauling the stuff to the island for shipment. As a consequence, word began to spread on the attractiveness of the area and its commercial potential. What she didn't learn was whether Susan and Wade Carson were currently residing on the island.

Tamra finished her meal. For dessert she strolled around the corner to the ice cream shop where she ordered two scoops of butter pecan in a cup. Once again, she took a seat to ponder her day, and more importantly, her tomorrow. She recalled the motto Adam had mounted on his desk: "You keep digging, you keep finding." Tomorrow, she would keep digging, just as determinedly as she was digging into the butter pecan in which she was finding great comfort.

"Hello, Tamra," said a calm, familiar voice from behind her.

She turned to face its source. "Wade!" she said, feigning surprise while covertly rejoicing in her luck.

THE MEMORIES CAME RUSHING BACK. Fresh out of college, Tamra and a longtime girlfriend by the name of Jan Palmer had decided to take a one-week beach break before they entered into the real world. On this occasion they sought out an isolated, peaceful locale rather than the honky-tonk atmosphere preferred by the party crowd. It was their little way of saying they were adults now, so let's start heading in that direction. At the time she had no way of knowing how significant a step it would be.

The manner in which they came to settle on Boca Grande as a destination was a simple one. They'd picked it out from a map. Their selection criteria were basic: Choose a place new to them, relatively close, on the water, and with an exotic history. The latter factor came at the request of her girlfriend, who unlike a growing number of their generation, took a great interest in geography and its historical backdrop. Jan viewed maps as the starting point for adventure. The place names alone were enough to stir her curiosity, none more than Boca Grande, though the exotic-sounding moniker was quickly reduced to the mundane when subjected to translation. "Big mouth," according to Jan, was more a description of a guy she once dated than a reference to the mouth of the waterway on the southern tip of the island. Nonetheless, the rudimentary reference did nothing to dampen their enthusiasm. Right away, they constructed a daily routine for the duration of the trip. By day they would stroll the beaches, and in the afternoon, shop the shops. In the evening they would dine at the converted railway station restaurant and, following that, cap off their evening with a stop around the corner at the ice cream stand.

For the entire week there was no interruption or variance to their routine...no intervention from a third party to disrupt two close friends from enjoying a girls' getaway. That was until their final sit-down for one last treat of ice cream to cap off the week.

"Excuse me...how are you at introductions?" the man at the table beside them leaned over to ask Jan.

Tamra received a quick glance from her girlfriend who served as the gatekeeper for the two when it came to men. The guy asking the question appeared a few years older; somewhere in his early to mid- twenties and indisputably handsome. He wore a sharp off-white outfit, from brimmed fedora hat and long-sleeved shirt, down to creased trousers and leather loafers. He also wore an easy smile on his tanned, chiseled face that let it be known he expected nothing other than a positive response.

Jan could have ended it there with a simple, "Sorry, I'm no good at introductions." However, she had already signaled to Tamra via her engaged eyes that she was not of a mind to close the gate. "Why do you ask?" she said in response.

"Because, if you don't introduce me to your girlfriend, this could easily turn out to be the worst night of my entire life," he answered, maintaining his confident smile. "Do you want to carry that around on your conscience for the rest of your entire life?"

"And if I do, who's to say it won't end up the worst night of her life?"

"I'll say it."

Tamra received another mirthful glance from her friend. She knew the gate was about to be swung wide open and the truth was she had no objection to it.

"Your name?" Jan asked the stranger.

"Wade...and yours?"

"Jan."

The gatekeeper turned to her companion who was nonchalantly working on her cup of ice cream. "Tamra, I'd like for you to meet Wade."

The smile on Wade's face broadened considerably as he reached out to take Tamra's extended hand. Moments later, at Jan's invitation, he was sitting at their table, engaging them in a conversation on the relative merits of the various flavors of ice cream and whether it's best to eat it from a cup or cone. As for his background, he was a Floridian by birth, a legal aid for now with designs on becoming a criminal attorney in the not too distant future. By evening's end he also had Tamra's phone number.

"You have to admit, he's dangerous looking in a good sort of way," Jan gushed to her friend on the way home.

She was half right, as Tamra later discovered during the courtship process. In the beginning the man did all the right things—took her to recitals, touring Broadway shows, movies, lectures, dinners—all the while behaving like a perfect gentleman. By most social measures it was a good start. The problem for her was in the pattern of activities that was developing. All were indoor...none were outdoor. For a woman who liked to dip her toes in the surf and explore the wilderness trails, it was a discouraging trend. On several occasions, she diplomatically suggested open-air alternatives, but they never seemed to get around to them. She also came to believe their outings were Wade's way of piling up personal investments in her which in turn ensured her becoming beholden to him on some level. On top of this was the total seriousness with which Wade viewed the world, from the grandest issues to the least significant. She liked to laugh and the men who could make her do so with their wit or self-deprecating humor definitely had a leg up on gaining her affections. The hokey line he used on Jan at the ice cream shop to elicit an introduction was as close to a jab at humor he had made since the night they met. Not that he was devoid of attributes, she confessed. A bit of a brooder, there was plenty of mystery lurking behind his manner, which admittedly intrigued her. Men from whom she could get a complete readout in a single sitting, held little interest for her---handsome or not. She enjoyed having to draw out a guy's deepest feelings in order for him to reveal himself. She once asked Wade what he looked for in a woman and his answer was immediate and typical in its murkiness—"The man in her."

"Does that mean I should be looking for the woman in you?" she asked in kind.

"Have at it. You might be surprised at what you find," he answered.

The whole looking for the man or woman in you eventually became a sore point in their relationship. Wade's bringing it up was a reference to author Preston Penrod's self-help book "The Consummate Intimacy: You in him...He in you," which had become the rage of the book world. Despite the book being aimed primarily at women, Wade had become a devotee of Penrod and his pop psychology, even to the point of trying to talk her into attending a local seminar on the fundamental tenets advanced by the author. That he would have to resort to the ramblings of a pop guru to build their relationship indicated to her a complete lack of confidence in his ability to connect with her on either an emotional or mental level. Where was that original bravado of his that he'd demonstrated at the ice cream shop?

"Be yourself," she told him in a fit of frustration at his attempt to reinvent himself on behalf of her. "The basic ingredients are all there, Wade. You don't need the advice of a third party to make a go of it. A little confidence in yourself will do." There came a point when she realized she was sounding either like a friend urging him on from the sidelines or a potential lover who was letting him know she was ripe for conquest. It was time to back off and let nature take its course, she decided.

In time, the digging for each other's true self became less a challenge than a chore. The getting-to-know-you stage had gone on long enough for her to conclude the two had no future together. At her core she was a blue-collar girl whose outlook on life was shaped by her father, a small trucking firm operator who died young but left her a lasting legacy of straight talk and common sense.

It was time to distance herself from Wade, she concluded. Unfortunately, the timing could not have been worse for her to begin the distancing. She was about to raise her concerns over dinner one night when Wade, possibly sensing he was on the brink of losing her, unexpectedly beat her to the punch by proposing to her. All she could think of at the time was. "Thank God it wasn't one of those stadium scoreboard proposals in front of thousands of onlookers that place an unfair burden on a woman." Still, the pressure weighed heavily, despite the obvious desperation of the move. Wade was waiting for a response and she was acting as though she was looking for the exit door. Perhaps she was the unfair one. The man deserved an answer to his question, after all.

"I think it may be time to take a step back, Wade," she lamely said to his proposal.

Her response took the life out of his eyes, momentarily leaving him bereft of words, something he was rarely short of. In their place came a brief flash of anger.

"Why, all of a sudden, the coolness?" he snapped. "As I've told you before, I grew up in a world of cold women, starting with my mother and continuing with a string of relationships with ice queens. You broke the pattern, Tamra. You were the first warm woman to come into my life."

"Because I'd rather live truthfully than in deceit," she determinedly replied to his question.

"And what is the truth?"

"The truth is I'm not sure at this point the feelings I have for you will ever evolve into love."

Wade leaned across the dinner table. "Are you willing to continue our relationship on the chance that in time that might occur?"

Tamra paused to collect her thoughts. "As I said, I believe for now it would be best for both of us to take a step back."

Ultimately, it was their careers that turned them in opposite directions or else out of habit they might have resumed the relationship following their so-called step back, which was more a wish on her part. Wade had decided to attend law school in Chicago. He felt strongly the relationship could be sustained in spite of the geographical divide. She, on the other hand, had her doubts, which proved to be true. Rather than their hearts growing fonder during the separation, they instead became restless and thus vulnerable to local pursuits, both personal and professional. What had begun with promise that evening at the ice cream stand eventually was lost, stranded somewhere in the distance between Tampa and Chicago. It would be another six years before fate, followed by a little plotting on her part, would bring them back together again.

––––––––

"MAY I JOIN YOU?" he asked politely.

"You may," she said, a jumble of feelings pulling her between the past and present.

He looked much the same, save for the five-o-clock shadow he was sporting and the noticeably drawn face, which, to her, added some character to it.

"Still favoring the butterscotch blend, I see," he said, sliding into the chair across from her.

"I've tried others, but always seem to come back to this," she said, setting aside her spoon. "Creature of habit, I suppose."

"What brings you down here?" he asked.

"A girl's getaway."

"One girl this time?"

"Just one."

He looked her directly in the eye. "I wouldn't have thought it possible, but you look more beautiful than ever."

He's going to make this mission very difficult, Tamra thought, fighting off the urge to parrot his words back and tell him she also wouldn't have thought it possible, but he looked more handsome than ever. "Thanks, but I've become very adept at covering things up."

"You're married?" he asked, observing her ring.

"Engaged."

"Lucky guy."

"Lucky gal...and you?" she asked in turn, noting his ring. "Married?"

He glanced at his finger. "Oh...yeah," he answered, as if it was the furthest thing from his mind.

"Is this a guy's getaway for you?"

"No, I actually live here now."

"How nice. The attorney business must be good," she said. "Surely, the bulk of your clients are not from here."

"What makes you think I'm an attorney?"

The answer caught her by surprise. "Sorry, I assumed an intelligent man like you would easily make it through law school," she said, covering her tracks.

He checked his watch. "Listen, I have to go and take care of some business. How long do you plan on staying?"

"Two days at the most."

"How about tomorrow morning we get together to finish this conversation?"

"Where?"

He pointed to the street they were on. "Head down this avenue until you hit First Street. Take a right and go another couple of blocks and you will run into the sea wall. I'll meet you there at nine. I live right up the street from it. "We'll sit and watch the waves for a while and then I'll show you my house. Okay?"

"Will your wife mind?"

He grinned. "We have what is commonly called an open marriage," he said, without the least bit of hesitation. "She won't mind at all."

Warning flags were popping up all over the place and not just for the stormy weather expected to hit in the next day or two. She had a thousand reasons to say no, yet a single one that trumped all the others. She had a client to be served.

"See you at nine," she said.

CHAPTER SIX

A ROADSIDE MARKER ALONG THE ACCESS ROAD LEADING TO THE Kansas interstate indicated the entrance ramp was a mile away. In a few minutes they would be back on the highway and up to speed—that was, if fate had not intervened. Halfway to the ramp, a tremor shook the bus. The driver at once slowed the vehicle and eased it to the shoulder of the road. "I'm going to see what that was," he announced to the passengers as he hurried to open the door and skip down the steps. Several minutes later he hopped back on board and explained they had a malfunctioning axle and would have to return to the Emporia station. A collective moan from the passengers, befitting the general looks of disappointment and frustration covering their faces, greeted the news. But what could they do other than accept the situation, albeit grudgingly? Having gingerly maneuvered the bus back to the Emporia station, the driver consulted with his superiors over the phone before informing those on board that a replacement vehicle was already on its way from Wichita.

"How long a wait?" the pony-tailed guy called out from the back.

"Same time it took us to get here...about an hour and a half. In the meantime, you are welcome to stay on board or stretch your legs outside if you wish. There are several chairs in the depot and benches outside the filling station next door. A little farther down there's a small cafe for those who'd like a coffee break. Sorry for the delay, but these things do happen, unfortunately."

The process of killing time had officially begun. Adam, along with most of the passengers, including Manny and the mob guy, chose to exit the bus.

Waiting around for something to happen was the default definition of the surveillance trade. Needless to say, Adam had plenty of experience in practicing it, though mostly from the front seat of a car or van and not in the middle of nowhere surrounded by spectators. The chances of something going awry this particular time were slim, he concluded. Manny and his pursuer were headed nowhere while the bus was disabled. What was a broke, scared kid from a faraway country to do? Call a cab to take him to KC or back to Wichita? Run to the highway and stick out a thumb? Head for the tall grass? Nope, for the time being they were all stuck in place, resigned to waiting for the game to resume.

Adam strolled down to the cafe for a cup or two of coffee. The rustic eatery's bare-bones exterior was made of wooden slate. A large plywood signboard attached to the front announced it was the Grassy Hills Cafe. The interior featured well-worn, rust-colored booths, a checkerboard brown-and-white tiled floor, and mustard-colored walls bearing license plates from what appeared at first glance to be all fifty states. Customers were few, the lunch brigade having yet to arrive. One booth was occupied by two highway patrolmen who were busy carrying on their profession's coffee-and-donuts tradition. A trio of older men sat at one end of the counter chattering at each other. Adam took a seat at the opposite end of it. A young, fresh-faced strawberry blond with long hair knotted in the back and a smile in her eyes promptly appeared out of nowhere to take his order.

"Are you with that broken-down bus?" she asked, pouring his brew.

"I'm afraid so."

"Same thing happened about six months ago right after I started working here."

"Good for business, huh?"

"That's what my boss says, but only if it occurs near mealtimes, not between them."

Adam glanced at a large black and gold pennant fastened on a wall behind the counter. "Let me guess...you're a student at Emporia State."

"Correct."

"What was the last book you read?"

"The last book I read? Is this some kind of a test?" she asked through an engaging smile equal to the one in her eyes. "I've never gotten that question from a customer before."

"I have a habit of asking women that question. It seems to jump-start the getting-acquainted process."

"Why women?

"They read more than men, so they can usually be counted upon to come up with an answer."

"Hey Natalie! How about a refill here?" a customer at the far end of the counter barked out.

"Excuse me a moment," she said, grabbing the coffee pot.

From where he sat, Adam had a good view through the cafe's large front window of the nearby bus station and its surroundings. Several passengers were still strolling about. Others already had found their landing spots, including Manny, who had parked himself on one of the benches fronting the filling station. The pony-tailed guy and accordion guy joined him a minute later. The kid still had a bewildered look on his face, as though he didn't know what to make of the circumstances that landed him in this faraway place.

The Pilgrim's Progress," Natalie said upon her return. "How about you?"

The Woman in White. I'm a sucker for old British mysteries."

"That's on one of my class reading lists!" she said excitedly.

Adam took a sip of the coffee...the fresh and robust kind

associated with diners. "How are you liking small town life?" he asked.

"Emporia is not a small town to me. I come from a much smaller one a little west of here."

"How small?"

"Last I checked the population was still under a thousand."

"You say a little west of here. Does that mean it sits in those hills I saw glimpses of coming in on the bus?"

"The Flint Hills...yes. Cottonwood Falls sits right in the middle of them," she said, grabbing a handful of silverware to wrap.

"There are waterfalls in Kansas?"

She laughed. "People are always asking that when they hear the town's name. Actually, the falls referred to are formed by a spillway running from nearby Chase Lake. There are three of them... multiple drops."

"How high?"

"They run maybe five to twenty feet high."

"Have you hiked the tall grass trails?"

"I consider it walking. Hiking to me is going up and down mountains. But, yes, I've walked them many times. It's part of growing up here."

"What is it that makes them special, Natalie?"

"The open sky...the fresh air...the scent of the wildflowers mixed in with the tall grass...the solitude of it all. It's almost like having a natural privacy fence running along each side of you during your walk."

As if on cue, distant strains of *"Red River Valley"* could be heard drifting in from outside the cafe. Through the window Adam noted the accordion guy showcasing his talent from the bench seat he occupied to a disinterested audience of captive passengers milling about. The disinterest extended to the mob guy who shunned taking a seat, preferring to pace around the grounds impatiently while puffing on a cigarette.

Adam returned his attention to Natalie. "The trails are long?" he asked.

"They're as long as you want to make them. You can blaze one of your own all the way to Nebraska, if you like," she said, snatching more silverware to wrap in preparation for the lunch crowd.

"You've hoofed it to Nebraska?"

"Nope. I've never been out of the state."

Adam cast her a quizzical eye. "You serious?"

"Friends call me either the anti-Dorothy or the wannabe Dorothy."

"What's the closest you've come?"

"Overland Park, Kansas, right near the Missouri border."

Adam eyed a message scribbled on a chalkboard attached to the wall behind the counter. "Special today...tuna of the plains...$5.95."

He gestured toward the sign. "You've got tuna swimming the streams around here?" he asked, drawing a chuckle from her.

"Prairie chicken...in these parts they are often referred to as the tuna of the plains," she informed him. "If you're stuck here long enough, you might give it a try for lunch."

"Hopefully, we will be well on our way by then."

The accordion guy ended his outdoor concert and conversed briefly with his two seatmates. Whatever was said caused all three to stretch their heads in every direction as though they were looking for someone.

The two highway patrolmen strode to the counter to pay their tabs. "Our server disappeared," one of them said.

"She's on her break," Natalie replied, stepping over to the register to check them out.

Adam watched them leave. So did mob guy. No sooner had they left than mob guy stubbed his cigarette into the ground and strolled into the café, stepping straight up to the counter. "You got a pay phone?" he asked of Natalie.

"Over there, near the pie case display," she said, pointing to a corner of the restaurant.

No booth, just a naked phone. Time to feast his eyes while practicing a little eavesdropping, Adam decided. Casually, he rose to his feet and ambled over to the display case where he was easily within earshot of the phone. Other than a dismissive glance, mob guy paid him no heed. He scanned the homemade pies on display---cherry, apple, coconut cream, and blueberry. They constituted a definite distraction for the pie lover he was, but he managed to set aside temptation to take in the jumble of words coming from the mob guy's mouth. "It'll have to be quick, Joey. We're running late as it is...Florida? Whereabouts? No, I sure as hell won't be taking a bus back to Vegas...right...right." Mob guy then hung up without saying goodbye to whomever was on the receiving end. He did flash Adam another look as he headed for the exit, this time one of annoyance, no doubt for encroaching on his space.

"You're not going to take one of the pies along with you?" Natalie asked Adam upon his return.

"No, but I'll settle for a piece of the coconut cream right now if you have one available."

"Sure do," she said and retrieved one from a small case behind the counter, pouring him more coffee at the same time. When he finished, he called for his tab. "Don't be the anti-Dorothy or wannabe Dorothy forever," he opined when paying it. Take a step over the boundary the next time you have the chance."

"You're obviously a more worldly person than I. In fact, most everyone is," she joshed.

"Does that qualify me to give you a second piece of advice?"

"Sure...I get plenty of it as it is around here, mostly from the locals."

"Well, here's a little suggestion from an outsider. There are going to be guys galore making proposals to you down the line, Natalie. Choose wisely. If I recall right from my school days, it was Aristotle who wrote the highest form of knowledge is wisdom... something to keep in mind, even for the younger generation."

She looked at him quizzically. "What do you do for a living?"

"You mean other than give random advice to strangers?"

"Yes...are you a teacher?"

"No, I track down bad guys for a living."

She gave him a cynical side eye. "On a bus?"

"Whatever works."

She turned her gaze past him and through the window to the

broken-down vehicle. "Whatever works?" she said, repeating his words with a wry smile.

———

THE REPLACEMENT BUS arrived and all passengers, at the encouragement of the driver, gravitated to the identical seats they occupied prior to the breakdown. A sense of relief that they may make it to Kansas City after all permeated the air as the vehicle entered the interstate. In keeping with the fresh optimism, accordion guy rose to the occasion and began to grind out a rollicking version of *"She'll Be Coming 'Round the Mountain."* A few more chords out of him and Adam was convinced the passengers would have been willing to pull an Agatha Christie and altogether do him in. The gallery of disapproving looks, however, was sufficient to squelch the music man's enthusiasm, leading him to cut short his spontaneous recital.

The subsequent silence on board, accented by the hypnotic whirr of the bus's tires, sent Adam into a reflective state into which drifted thoughts of Tamra. He wondered how she was doing on her case. It seemed a simple one on the surface, yet domestic disputes, as he had learned from previous cases and talking to cops, could flare up instantly, placing third party interventionists in peril.

Yes, he was having serious second thoughts on their little experiment of both working separate cases simultaneously. There was something to be said—much to be said as a matter of fact—for someone holding down the fort while the other was away doing the legwork. Perhaps the growth of cell phone usage could help in this regard. He would have Tamra look into it once they were finished with the two cases. She had been, after all, lobbying for it for some time.

A warm shaft of sunlight streaming through the window fell across Adam's face and upper torso, transporting him into a deeper reverie, replete with more personal reflections on his future wife, the thoughts eventually lulling him into a comforting sleep.

———

A WAILING siren from a passing highway patrol car was the first warning of additional trouble awaiting them on the road to KC. The piercing sound woke Adam from his slumber. *Okay, they're chasing down a speedster*, he first thought, an observation he at once dismissed when two other vehicles flew by close on the heels of the patrol car. Both had electronic gear sprouting every which way from their frames. To Adam they resembled moon rovers, though he knew full well what they were from TV documentaries he had seen—storm chasers.

He peered out the window toward the southern horizon. Dark clouds were mobilizing, churning menacingly, as if preparing for a large-scale ground assault. The leading edge of the cloud cover by this time had eclipsed the sun, darkening the entire landscape.

"Any idea how far we are from KC?" he asked the pony-tailed guy seated a row ahead of him across the aisle.

"About forty miles," he answered, keeping his eyes fixed in the same concerned manner as the other riders on the weather event unfolding a relatively short distance away. "A couple up front have a portable radio. They said the weather forecasters are calling for tornado activity in the region. Looks like they may have called this one right," he added. He then reached his hand out across the aisle to Adam. "Cory Hoagland," he said as a way of introduction. "Adam Fraley," came the response in like fashion.

Another storm chasing vehicle came racing past the bus. This one was running low to the ground and sporting a makeshift protective metal shield covering its front frame. A guy hung out one of its windows with camera in hand, ready to capture evidence of the storm's wrath should it occur, like a passenger bus getting tossed into a ditch.

Adam eyed the bus driver who appeared nonplussed, despite the situation confronting him. He could empathize with the guy, having served a short stint as a bus driver while in the Air Force. He was between assignments at the time and to give him something to do, the brass temporarily attached him to the motor pool. Occasionally, he ended up behind the wheel of a bus, hauling military personnel and dependents around the base or into town for various functions. He had his share of incidents to deal with, though none rose to the level of the one presently facing the guy up front.

Recalling his military training, Adam inserted himself into the mind of the driver. What to do? First, check with the home office. Let them know the situation. "Whatever you do, make sure the safety of your passengers is your top priority," would likely be the reply, "Only take the action you deem most appropriate." Wouldn't the most appropriate action be to pull to the side of the road and wait? For what? Might as well keep chugging along in the slim hope a safe haven would magically appear in the direction they were headed.

All eyes were on the thick, black slow-moving cloud mass presently hanging low and threateningly above them. If anything were to happen, there was no better chance of it than now, Adam figured. When it did, the unpredictability of it would become a stark reality. From the centermost point of the cloud cover appeared a rotating motion. Moments later, a funnel spiraled down from its innards, touching ground not a mile away from the road they were traveling. The sight drew a gasp from the passengers. No sooner had the twister touched down and begun its spewing of debris than a loud, continuous blast from an air horn, equivalent to a sour high note emanating from a pipe organ, shook the passengers.

Heads swiveled from the windows to the front of the bus. The driver was slumped over the wheel with his arms stretched across the control panel. Adam assumed one of the guy's arms had landed on the air horn activator. He rushed up the aisle, followed by Cory Hoagland, the accordion guy, and the Hispanic man. He grabbed the steering wheel with one hand, simultaneously raising the driver's upper torso with the other, silencing the air horn. "Can you get him to an empty seat so I can jockey this thing," he said to the other two. The men half carried and half dragged the passed-out driver to a vacant seat where one of the female students tended to him. "I'm a nursing major," she professed. Meanwhile, Adam took command of the vehicle. Thanks to the relatively straight stretch of highway they were traveling, the bus had veered no more than a few feet off the shoulder of the road during the exchange. He hurriedly steered the vehicle back onto the roadway. Once settled, he returned his attention to the twister.

"Why don't you park this damn thing on the side of the road and wait it out?" the mob guy barked from behind him. At the moment the funnel appeared to be headed directly their way, though that could change from one moment to the next. Even a guy from South Florida knew that much. The twister's width was fifty yards, he estimated, and was moving in a northeasterly direction. It was going to intersect with the highway---but where, exactly? He was never good at those math teasers in school, the ones that asked if a train leaves Chicago for Los Angeles at 10:00 a.m. central time at 75 miles per hour and another leaves Los Angeles for Chicago at 10:00 a.m. west coast time at 60 miles per hour, at what time do they meet in the middle? He was in the sixth grade at the time. How the hell should he know? All he knew was that the twister and their bus were headed on a collision course.

As the tornado drew nearer, the noise level rose dramatically along with the air pressure. As veterans of such storms had pointed out in the past, the roar was similar to that of an approaching freight train, loud enough in this instance to drown out conversation within the bus.

Adam was certain one last vision of the overhanging specter would stay with him forever, that was, if he lived to tell it. The Kansas sun was attempting to break through the overcast, coloring the rotating clouds into various shades of gray, ultimately forming the vision of a mammoth elephant's head with its long snout sweeping back and forth across the terrain in a bellicose manner. And to think the mammal was a childhood favorite of his, he nervously gibed to himself.

He was about to slam on the brakes and give up the catch-me-if-you-can game when he caught out of the corner of his eye a rise in the road directly ahead. From the top of the rise to the base of the roadbed, he estimated to be a drop of twenty-five feet. With the twister on a southwesterly to northeasterly path, he needed to cross to the northern side of the rise to reach the potential safe haven.

As if the approaching twister itself was not generating enough concern, another problem at once grabbed his attention, causing him to slow the bus to a crawl.

"Why are we stopping?" a voice shouted from the rear of the bus.

A short distance ahead, afore the rise, a batch of loosened high-tension wires from a downed power line were flailing all about like giant whips. One wire was dancing back and forth on the road's surface, trailing a shower of sparks. He knew not to drive over it on the chance the line would get caught up in the tire treads and possibly loop around the axle, electrifying the bus to the tune of about 350,000 volts of energy. The moment Adam halted the bus, the wire ceased its dancing. It lay motionless, coiled across the pavement like a snake ready to strike. Adam's choice was to wait and hope the twister veered off the course it was traveling or take his chances and drive across the tension line.

"Come on...come on," he whispered under his breath in a last-second plea for the line to whip back off the road.

His plea was answered when a burst of wind from the advancing twister sent the line skidding off the highway. He had his opening. Now was the time to make his move.

He grabbed the PA System mike. "Buckle your seat belts," he shouted through the clamor to the passengers.

As he passed the downed wires thrashing dangerously close to the shoulder of the road, he carefully maneuvered the vehicle off the highway to the side opposite them, buck-boarding across the meridian, over the parallel highway, and down the incline, toward the ditch at the base of the embankment. Debris was shooting every which way, as he guided the vehicle to a stop flush up against the side of the rise. He turned off the engine and glanced around to see if there were any signs of flames or smoke, indicating a stealth strike by the wires. There were none. All they could do now was sit and wait. There was nothing left to do other than see if they could outlive the storm.

The winds swept across the rise, buffeting the bus, despite its earthen shield. Uprooted trees shot horizontally across the road, while wooden planks were tossed against fences. Far afield a lone cow could be seen swishing its tail while munching on grass, oblivious to the event, as if refusing to allow the storm to interrupt its contentment. At one point he felt the bus lifting and simultaneously the windows starting to bow, signaling the vehicle was about to implode from the air pressure. Fortunately, it held together and for the most part remained intact. But where was the funnel? The answer was found in the rearview mirror---one hundred yards or so behind them, factoring in the admonition, "Objects may be closer than they appear." It crossed at nearly the exact spot where he had hit the brakes to avoid the downed power line. The twister was still in view as it continued on its northeasterly path.

In short order, the winds subsided, as the tornado exited the stage followed by the rains, something Adam knew would pose another potential threat. A downpour would likely leave them stuck in the mud. The idea of having to wait for another replacement bus was too much to bear. He ignited the engine and carefully guided the vehicle up the embankment, across the westbound lane, over the meridian to the shoulder of the eastbound lane where he again shut the engine down to let things settle. Amid the aftermath of the twister's passing, the toddler on board began to cry, a poignant reminder to all of how precious and precarious life can be.

———

THEY WERE NOT the only ones parked along the road. Storm chasers had converged on the scene with cameras in tow. One chaser hustled over through the rain and rapped on the door. He had doubtless seen the bus emerge from out of nowhere and was primed with questions. "Were you driven off the road by the twister?" he shouted. "How did you end up in the ditch? Where are you headed? Any damage to the vehicle? Anyone hurt?" Adam waved him off. If the other passengers were of a like mind, they also were in no mood to be peppered with questions. He kept the door closed.

Adam felt a tap on his shoulder. "I can take over from here," the regular driver said, surprising him. "Good job by you." He looked past him to the student nurse. "He's okay," she mouthed to him. Apparently, he had just passed out, Adam surmised. "It's all yours," he said to the driver, hopping down from his perch to return to his seat. Along the way, he received a couple of high fives and pats on the back. Once settled in his seat, he returned his attention to Manny and the mob guy, both of whom sat as they were before all the commotion started. In a way it was probably a welcome diversion for the kid, away from thoughts of what might await him at the end of the ride. In Adam's mind the task for him was to see to it that the end game was one neither the mob guy nor Manny had in mind.

CHAPTER SEVEN

For the next thirty to forty minutes, the bus played tag with the tail end of the storm system, as both continued on a north by northeasterly track. Eventually, the rains dissipated and by the time they reached the outer KC suburb of Olathe the skies had cleared. Adam looked to the front of the bus at the mob guy and Manny. Their body language signaled a heightened restlessness in both of them. It also conveyed to him the need to finalize his plan to separate the two.

He settled on a simple strategy to reduce the risk of something going haywire. He carried in his shirt pocket the photo of Manny that Timmy had given him. In the picture's background stood an older man and woman, each with a hand resting on Manny's shoulders. Undoubtedly, they were his parents. He viewed the photo as his passport to an intervention. When the time came, he would walk up and flash it to Manny, at the same time informing him he was here at the request of his parents to bring him home safely. Unless he was mistaken, Manny would jump at the chance to head in a different direction. As for the mob guy, Adam had the element of surprise on him. By the time he will have realized what had happened, Manny will have been whisked away, leaving mob guy in the lurch with no good explanation for his bosses on how it all came about. Of course, there was always the possibility the mob guy wasn't a mob guy. In that case he would simply take Manny by the arm and escort him home.

Adam first became aware of a KC-Vegas underworld connection thanks to another brief Air Force experience. While stationed in Tampa, he was assigned to take a one-week seminar on base security at Richards-Gabauer Air Force Base on the Missouri side of the metro area. During his time there, he read a lengthy article in the local paper on the history of Kansas City's notorious crime figures. A political boss by the name of Tom Pendergast got the ball rolling on the city's road to perdition. The Pendergast machine ruled the city for the entire Prohibition era. He turned the town into a wide-open underworld playground, seeing to it that there were no alcohol arrests throughout the period of the ban. Following in the footsteps of the Pendergast machine were the mob families, born in the city's Italian district. They emerged as the kingpins of organized crime in the area and in time took their operations a step further, by using their influence with the Teamsters Union to build casinos in Las Vegas. They financed their operations with revenue from the union's pension fund. Not only did they build the casinos, they skimmed them until state and federal authorities shut down their activities. The article ended with the observation that the history of crime families showed they were rarely vanquished completely. When their operations were exposed or their don faced jail time, there were always uncles, sons, cousins, or nephews waiting in the wings to carry on the tradition. Adam wondered: *Was it too far-fetched to believe not all of the Vegas connections had been rooted out? Was it reasonable to conclude Manny got caught up in one of the family's residual gambling operations and was about to pay the price for it?*

Adam again noticed Manny nervously glancing over his shoulder toward the back of the bus while studiously avoiding direct eye contact with the mob guy. "Yeah, he's still there, kid, and he isn't going anywhere for now," Adam murmured under his breath.

From Olathe the bus continued on its exurban-suburban trek through the posh towns of Lenexa, Merriam, and Mission Hills, before crossing into Missouri and onto a freeway headed north. "Let's see...there's a Kansas City, Missouri and a Kansas City, Kansas," Adam mused aloud. "To really confuse things, they should rename Kansas City, Kansas to Missouri City, Kansas, then you would have a Kansas City, Missouri and a Missouri City, Kansas, all in cozy proximity to each other."

The freeway led them past several noteworthy sites---a World War I memorial, a soaring bluff with an impressive statue of an Indian scout riding a horse mounted atop it, the headquarters of Hallmark Cards, a restored railway union station, and finally to the eastern edge of the downtown district where the bus depot was located. From there it was a short distance to the North End Italian neighborhoods, in which was hatched the Las Vegas connection, Adam recalled from the article he had read when stationed nearby.

Nearing its destination, the bus slowed to execute a long loop around an industrial block. At the far end of the loop stood the off-road station. Showtime in the show-me state was about to commence, Adam reckoned.

ADAM PROMPTLY SURVEYED the scene upon their arrival. To his delight it was a hub of activity. Four buses were parked at the loading gates. On the access street outside the complex, several taxis, along with an airport shuttle van, were positioned for a rush of customers. All were viable options for him to beat a hasty exit from the grounds with Manny in tow. The bad news was something he should have anticipated but didn't. In addition to all the other vehicles, there were two news crews camped out on the site. The bus driver no doubt had passed word ahead to his superiors of the twister episode, he surmised. In turn, the media got wind of it, rendering his grab-and-go strategy less foolproof by the minute.

The bus eased to a stop at the arrival gate. Straight away,

passengers scrambled to gather their carry-on belongings. This was one bus they could not wait to abandon. Adam figured few of them had bags stored in the luggage bin under the carriage. Without appearing rude he deftly stepped around distracted passengers to the front of the bus directly behind Manny and his pursuer who had moved to the head of the line. *Why would he do that?* Adam wondered. *"Why not stay directly behind his prey, so as not to lose sight of him?"*

The driver blew open the door and the exiting began, led by the mob guy with Manny and Adam closely trailing. The moment they entered the bustling terminal lobby, the news crews descended upon them.

"Who was the passenger who took over the bus during the storm?" one of the reporters shouted at the first man off the bus. Mob guy, whether instinctively or deviously, turned and pointed straight at Adam who at once became the center of attention. The next thing he knew he had two microphones stuck in his face.

"Are you the man who took command of the bus during the storm?" a reporter asked him.

"Yes," he snapped, as he attempted to weave his way through the gathering throng.

"What were the circumstances that led you to do it?" another reported called out over the clamor, while scrambling to keep up with him.

"The regular driver should be along in a minute. He can fill you in on all the details," he responded, begging off further questioning.

In short order, he weaved through the crowd, frantically looking for the mob guy and Manny, whom he'd lost sight of in the crush. In a scene that jarred him, he spotted ahead his underworld suspect surrounded by several children and two adult women. Two of the kids were holding up makeshift signs reading, "Welcome home Uncle Sal." If he'd had the time or agility, Adam would have given himself a quick kick in the butt. Instead, he hustled down the lobby, past a cluster of vending machines and a game room packed with kids to the ticket counters. If he was wrong on "Uncle Sal," he could be just as mistaken on Manny not continuing his journey by bus clear to Tampa. Alas, there was no Manny at the ticket stations.

He took one more look around the lobby, before bolting out of the terminal's main entrance, just in time to discover he was half right regarding the entire scheme of events. At the far end of the parking lot sat a late model black van. There stood Manny next to an open rear door. On one side of him was Cory Hoagland who had him gripped by the arm. To his other side was the accordion guy who had in his grasp the other arm. They were in the process of shoving him into the back of the vehicle.

"Hey!" Adam bellowed out to them, as he sprinted in their direction. All three turned to look at the interloper, but he was too late. Manny disappeared into the back seat along with his captors. An instant later, the van made a sharp U-turn and sped away at too far a distance and at an unfortunate angle for him to get a license plate number.

He stood in the middle of the parking lot, his overnight bag hanging limply from his arm. He swore to the skies and then at himself. How often had his former boss and long-time mentor advised him of the dangers of stereotyping. "It will blind you as sure as a cup of acid to the eyes," he had warned.

Adam trudged back to the terminal a chastened man. There he was greeted for a second time by the news crews.

———

FOLLOWING another give-and-take session with the reporters, this one conducted on a more cordial level, Adam hopped a cab to the downtown central police station. The desk sergeant, a woman with a no-nonsense demeanor, at once cast a wary eye at the overnight bag he was carrying. "What do you have there?" she asked.

"Dirty clothes."

"Are you sure it isn't a dirty bomb?"

Adam zipped open the bag and showed her the proof. She, in turn, checked the name tag.

"What can we do for you, Mr. Fraley?"

He gave her a shortened version of his story in keeping with the overt disinterest she had on display. Nevertheless, she grabbed the desk phone and dialed an extension. "You got time to listen to a civilian's account of a possible abduction...okay...I'll send him in. His name is Adam Fraley. He's carrying a satchel. Disregard it." She replaced the phone and turned her disinterest back to Adam. "Follow this hallway down to the last room on the right. Sergeant Kendall will be expecting you."

The room was your standard police bullpen, containing close to two dozen desks, a third of them occupied at the moment. Kendall was a tall, slender cop somewhere in his thirties with a buzz cut and a manner in direct contrast to the gatekeeper out front. The sergeant led him to his desk, pointing to the chair fronting it. "Have a seat. I hear you have a possible abduction to report."

Adam gave his account of the incident, a more detailed one this time around. All the while, the hum of office activity continued unabated in the background.

"Mr. Fraley, I'm going to be blunt right up front," the sergeant said on hearing his account. "For us to take up a missing person case, the request best come from a family member. That's not to say there are no exceptions, but those are rare. Secondly, your Manny is legally an adult. Unless it's clearly evident he's in immediate danger of some kind, there is no reason to expend our resources on trying to track him down. As things stand, you have no license plate number, nor any names of the purported abductors...."

"Oh, but I do have one name—Cory Hoagland. You could have the passenger list checked for him," Adam interjected.

The sergeant cast him a cynical smile. "Mr. Fraley, don't you think those two guys likely considered that possibility beforehand and chose to give false identifications? Let's say all of which you state is true and I have no reason to doubt it. That still leaves us with a hurdle we can't clear—the jurisdictional one. Manny is a foreign student who's gone missing...a young guy presumably involved in an interstate gambling operation. This is a matter for the Feds. I suggest you ask Manny's parents to contact the FBI office in Tampa for help in finding him. As for the Kansas City-Las Vegas crime connection, there may be splinter groups still operating in one form or the other, yet nothing on the scale they once did."

The attention of both men was drawn to a mobile TV stand positioned near the entrance to the room. One of the bullpen crew had turned up the sound on the unit mounted atop it. The reason was readily apparent. The guy sitting at Kendall's desk was the same guy fielding questions from reporters. "Passenger takes over bus during tornado strike. Tune in at six for the story," was the headline crawling across the bottom of the screen.

Kendall glanced at the monitor. "You're now a local celebrity," he said with a grin.

Adam shrugged his shoulders. Celebrity status was the furthest thing from his mind.

"Like I said, Mr. Fraley. This is a case for the Feds." Words that ended the conversation. He was right, Adam reluctantly concluded, leaving him with the lasting vision of a bewildered Manny as he was being shoved into the back end of a van and hauled away to who knows where.

———

ADAM HAILED a taxi to take him to the airport. In a last-ditch effort to pick up the trail of Manny, he asked the driver to swing by the North End for a brief neighborhood tour. He claimed to be an out-of-towner who had a fixation with crime families, having devoured every book and article he could get his hands on detailing their activities.

"This place isn't what it used to be," the driver proclaimed in a bass voice that blended well with his gruff exterior.

They were cruising the neighborhood, comprised mainly of vintage commercial structures built within sight of the Missouri River winding its way through the downtown area.

"A bunch of high-minded political reformers wanted to drive a stake through the mob establishment so they built a major freeway right through the heart of this place. As a result, the neighborhood became literally divided, paving the way for an influx of other ethnic groups, especially the Vietnamese following the war over there. I guess you could say there was little assimilation among the groups. Everyone wanted to maintain their way of life, including the Italians, so they stuck to their own neighborhoods."

As the driver waxed on, Adam casually eyed the streets. He knew the chances of spotting accordion guy or Cory Hoagland, much less the black van they were riding in, were nearly non-existent. "By chance, have you ever seen an accordion player and pony-tailed guy walking these streets together?" he asked from the back seat of the cab.

"Accordion player? Hell, this is the land of Sinatra, Damone, and Caruso. Plenty of the pony-tailed types but, nope, never seen such a combo together and I'm in and out of this area quite a bit."

"So, you're familiar with the neighborhood."

"Way back when, I went to school with kids from the North End. Great guys who would give you the shirt off their back if you asked. You cross them, though, and they take the skin off yours. I recall in high school once going to a prom dance with one of the kids from a so-called crime family. They hired two guards to accompany us in the limo."

"Crossing them...like sticking them with an unpaid gambling debt?"

"Bingo! I've often wondered about the kids from these mob families. Many of them are sent by their parents to the finest schools...private ones in many cases. And for what? To become doctors? Lawyers? Never heard of a doctor or lawyer that was an offspring of a mafia guy. Sure, there might be some. I'm just not aware of any. A few of the kids I knew didn't even seem aware of the illegal stuff their families were involved in. The parents kept it hidden from them."

"And those that do become aware...how many try to break with the tradition and refuse to follow in their father's footsteps or else try their hand at different kinds of crime?" Adam asked.

"Hard to escape from the family influence," the cabby

countered. "You've heard of the old saying 'God, family, and country.' Well, with them it's family, God, and the politicians you own, and that's it."

Adam spotted a sign—'Columbus Square Park.' "Appropriate name for a park in this area."

"Yeah, some people refer to this whole area as Columbus Square."

"Why?"

"It goes back to the time when this was a tight-knit community. In those days the locals looked out for each other...respected their heritage. To this day the residential streets reflect it. Many of the houses back up to each other with tall privacy fences between them. It allows the residents to go from house to house without being seen. Rumors were there were also tunnels between the homes. Remember when The Godfather movie came out?"

"Sure."

"An Italian organization here bought up all the local theater's opening night tickets and made a big show of disposing them. The action was intended to send the message they didn't approve of Hollywood's portrayal of their community. Of course, many of the locals ended up seeing it elsewhere."

Adam noted the name of the driver posted on the dashboard. "Say, Robert, can I ask a favor of you?"

"You can always ask. Doesn't mean you're going to get the answer you want."

"Can you drop me off here and come back, say, in an hour, to pick me up? There'll be an extra tip in store for you. I'd like to take a short stroll through the neighborhood. See what it's all about...maybe capture some of the flavor of it."

"You got a deal. I have to run an errand, anyway. I'll drop you off at Junior's Deli up the street. Meet you in front of it in an hour."

The deli was housed in a faded white brick building. A green and white striped awning stretched the length of it. Other than the coffee and coconut cream pie in Emporia and a couple of energy bars he had pocketed for the trip, Adam had eaten nothing. A deli sandwich was definitely in order, he decided. After Robert dropped him off, he made a beeline toward the eatery's entrance.

A chubby, bald-headed man wearing a white apron greeted him from behind the counter. "What's you pleasure?" he asked, as Adam scanned the menu posted on the wall.

"How about one of those salami sandwiches on rye and an Italian soda," he responded.

"Any condiments?"

"A little mayo is all."

"Here or to go?"

"Here will be fine."

The clerk slapped the sandwich together, placed it on a small paper plate, and handed it and the bottled drink over the counter to him.

"Thanks... I take it you're familiar with the neighborhood here," he said to the clerk.

"Born-and-bred familiar," came the reply.

"I'm just passing through. I met two guys a while back who I believe are from this area. One is named Cory Hoagland. He's a lanky, pony-tailed guy. The other fellow's name escapes me for the moment. He has a medium build and is always carrying around a hand-held accordion which he likes to play incessantly. Ever see such a twosome?"

"Nope...not that I recall," he said in a dismissive manner.

"Where's all your business this evening?" Adam asked aloud, as he took a seat at one of the dozen or so tables covered with red and white checkerboard table cloths. At once, he questioned the propriety of his query, realizing it could easily be considered a dig.

"Slow day today," came the stock reply.

Slower it couldn't get. Presently, he was the sole customer in the place. No sooner had he noted it than an elderly, matronly woman entered through the front door.

"Mrs. Fontana...good to see you," the clerk called out in a warm greeting.

"Hello Frankie," she said, shuffling over to the counter with purse in hand. "Can you slice me a half pound of pepperoni and a half pound of salami? I'm short on both."

"Be glad to," he said and went to work on the order.

Meantime, Adam was munching on his sandwich while taking in the interior decor of the store, replete with photos of Italian celebrities and scenes from the old country.

Frankie finished Mrs. Fontana's order and checked her out, wishing her an *"arrivederci"* on her way out the door.

Adam glanced at a wall clock. He still had forty minutes to walk the neighborhood while it was still light outside. He hurriedly finished off his sandwich and drink, paid his bill, and with a replenished stomach, took to the streets. He strolled down a side avenue to the residential district and made a left turn at the first block he came upon. Like the taxi driver pointed out, many of the houses backed up to each other with privacy fences between them. Front porches with flower pots on display were another common feature, as were the finely manicured lawns fronting them.

He had trekked no longer than halfway down the street when all at once he heard the cry of a woman a short distance away. He spotted her two houses down. It was Mrs. Fontana. She was bent over on a front sidewalk leading to what he assumed was her house. Her bag of groceries lay at her feet. She must have tripped and dropped it, he surmised. In a trice, he rushed to her side.

"Are you okay, ma'am?" he asked, noting no visible injuries to her.

"Yes...I must have stumbled over a crack in this sidewalk. Not surprising...it's as old as me after all."

Adam glanced at the walk and found it to be crack free, a finding he kept to himself.

"Could you help me with the groceries?"

"Sure."

Adam snatched the paper bag from the sidewalk, as well as the two wraps of meat products which had spilled from the container. Her purse she had managed to hold on to. He placed the meat wraps back in the bag and handed it to her.

"Ma...what's going on!"

A man dressed in jogging sweats had darted from the side of the house and rushed toward the two. He wasted no time accosting Adam, shoving him backward with both hands.

"What the hell are you doing?" he shouted at Adam. He was a strapping guy with a thick mane of hair and thicker muscles, the kind of man you wanted on your side in any physical confrontation. Nonetheless, Adam was prepared to defend himself should there be a second shove. "Hold on there," he said to the guy.

"Gino...Gino!" the mother snapped to her son. "He was just trying to help me."

Gino was in no mood to listen to his mother. He was far more interested in confronting the guy he deemed her mugger.

"What are you doing in this neighborhood?" he barked.

"Visiting."

"Visiting? Visiting who?"

"Visiting the neighborhood. I enjoy exploring old ethnic neighborhoods. It's an old hobby of mine," he said, before realizing how lame and mocking his explanation might come across.

"How did you get here?" growled Gino.

"Taxi."

"Hey Gino—you need help over there?" a next-door neighbor called out from his porch.

"Nah, I can handle it."

"Gino...get in the house," his mother commanded.

"Not until this jerk gets off our property," he responded.

"Okay...okay," Adam said, raising his hands in a gesture of appeasement. It was his property, after all.

"Ma'am," he said, bowing his goodbye to Mrs. Fontana, before turning to leave.

"Thank you," he heard her say, allowing him to depart in a somewhat cordial manner.

His enthusiasm for exploring the neighborhood having been drained by the incident, Adam opted to return to the deli to await Robert.

On his trek back, his attention was drawn to a narrow alleyway that ran behind the deli. He hadn't paid much heed to it on his stroll to the residential section. Upon his return, however, he caught from the corner of his eye a man standing behind a dark Lincoln Continental whose trunk lid was popped wide open. The man appeared to be lining the trunk with what looked like a white bed sheet. The man glanced over his shoulder at Adam who nonchalantly continued on his way.

If the deli clerk was surprised by his return visit, he wasn't demonstrating it. From the blank expression on his face, it was as though he were expecting him back all along. He ordered a cup of coffee and retired to the same table he occupied earlier. Once again, he was the sole customer in the place—not for long, however. Four middle-aged men, all bearing a neighborhood air about them, strolled into the store and instead of heading to the counter to order, walked straight to a table at the rear of the dining area to settle in. The clerk saw the four yet made no effort to engage them in conversation. Adam had only a side-eye view of them from where he sat. Over the next several minutes, he noticed them casually glancing his way, yet saying nothing to him, nor the clerk, nor most disturbingly, to one another. Adam bided his time, focusing on the street out front. Robert should be making an appearance any minute now and the last thing he wanted to do was miss his ride.

As if on cue, Frankie strode from behind the counter over to the entrance to momentarily fiddle with the door latch, before heading back to the counter.

Did he just lock us in?

Adam felt like he had been dropped into the middle of a Martin Scorsese film. The image of the man lining the car trunk behind the store came immediately to mind. At any moment he expected a camera crew to silently appear out of the blue and someone to shout out "action." He determined right then and there he was going to stick to his own script. He took a last swig of coffee, walked over and placed the empty cup on the counter along with the money to cover the cost and headed for the door. As he half expected, it was locked. He looked for the clerk who was nowhere to be seen. He next looked to the four men sitting in the back who were all eyeing him with stone faces. He was about to unlatch the door himself when Frankie appeared from a back room.

"Your door's locked," Adam said impassively.

"Sorry," Frankie said, tossing aside the dish towel he had in hand. "It's past closing time. We do it to keep people out, not to lock customers in," he said through a forced grin.

The clerk unlatched the door to let him out. *"Arrivederci,"* he said.

Before Adam stepped out the door, he glanced at the four men at the back table, one of whom raised his hand to wave him a fake goodbye.

A wimpy ending, a happy ending, or a nothing ending, he wasn't sure. Whichever, he would take it.

Robert was waiting for him outside. "How did it go?" he asked.

"You know...I'm not sure. Could have been worse...could have been better."

"Anything else you want to see?" the driver asked. "If so, you'd better hurry or else you're going to miss your flight."

It dawned on Adam he was on a fool's mission. All he was doing was dawdling, hoping for a miracle, and what private investigator made a living doing that?

"You're right. Enough of this...time to head for the airport."

———

THE ERRANT NORTH END episode nearly caused Adam to miss his flight to Tampa. However, that wasn't the biggest near miss of the day. They had just pulled to a stop at the airport terminal when the driver uttered the magical words to awaken him from his funk. "This isn't the North End, but right over there is a pony-tailed guy and another fellow carrying an accordion headed out of the terminal."

Adam hurriedly snatched his billfold from a back pocket to pay the driver, adding a generous tip. Grabbing his satchel, he flew out the door and sprinted toward the two men who were headed toward a taxi. He reached them before they had a chance to enter it. "Where's Manny?" he shouted to them, freezing the two in their tracks. The looks of surprise on their faces at seeing him were equal to his own at finding them.

"Who's Manny?" Cory Hoagland asked, his hand on the cab door.

"Don't give me that crap," Adam retorted. "You know damn good and well who he is. I saw you get into the van with him back at the bus station...or should I say I saw you and your buddy shove him into it."

"Oh, that was his name?" the accordion guy responded with a phony quizzical look on his face. "The kid said he needed a ride to the airport, so we asked the guy who was giving us one if he could take on another rider. He said, 'sure.'"

"The driver of the black van said that?"

"Yep," accordion guy replied.

"Well...where's the van and where's he?"

"Long gone, as far as we know," Hoagland answered, swinging open the cab door.

"And why did you need a ride to the airport?" Adam pressed on. "Not for a plane ride I take it."

"Listen, we don't have to answer to you," Hoagland said, opening the cab's back door for both of them to enter. "Whoever or whatever you're after is no business of ours."

For an instant Adam considered tailing them in another cab but decided the better move was to focus on Manny. It was possible that he was taken to the airport and turned over to whomever would take him on a flight to wherever. There was a chance the flight had yet to take off, so he decided to check as many departure gates as he could before his own flight started boarding. He could always reschedule to a later flight, if need be.

Adam half sprinted from one boarding gate to another in the time he had left. At one point he passed his own flight preparing to board. How fortunate would it have been to see Manny sitting there, with or without escorts, but no such luck. Hurrying onward, he spotted an airport information center. He asked the clerk if she could page a foreign student by the name of Manny Rivera to come to the desk. It was an emergency, he claimed. She agreed to do so and seconds later he heard her transmitting the request over the intercom. The chances of Manny responding were slim, he realized, particularly if a goon or two were escorting him. Even so, there was the chance one of the goons, solely out of curiosity, would respond to the paging.

Adam took a seat where he could observe the information desk from a distance without being noticed. He then waited...and waited...and still no Manny. *The kid is gone*, he concluded. If only he had not taken that detour to the North End, he might have been sitting here when Manny and his escorts arrived. As he second-guessed himself, he heard over the speaker system the announcement his flight was boarding. The brutal truth was he was going home empty handed, accompanied only by the strains of *Red River Valley* as performed by the accordion guy, echoing in his ears.

CHAPTER EIGHT

Tamra sat on a ledge atop the seawall, her gaze fixed on the great expanse of the Gulf. A stiff morning wind was churning the waters, hurling row after row of waves crashing onto the shore.

"Nice view, isn't it?"

She didn't need to turn to see whose question it was. "I can't imagine anyone disagreeing," she replied, feeling his presence.

"Have you spotted any dolphins?" he asked, coming to a stop behind her. "They often come out to play in the morning."

"No, but I did see an iguana over there in the shrubs. Are they still considered a nuisance around here?"

"Oh, yeah...they're considered an invasive species. The town has become a battleground between the residents and the reptile. Some locals armed with BB guns have even taken to patrolling the streets in golf carts. What the iguana hunters need and are not going to get this time of the year is a good cold snap."

"How does that help?"

"During a frigid cold, iguanas slow down and eventually become immobile. To try and escape it, they will often take to the trees where they become comatose. It's not unusual for them to lose their grip and start tumbling to the ground once they reach that state. If they're lucky, they will thaw out as soon as the sun comes back out. Otherwise, the environmental people will rush to round them up and haul them away."

"Let's hope some kind of living arrangement is reached between the two," she said. "I would hate for the town to lose its reputation as a peaceful little paradise."

"If I had a couple of BB guns stashed away from my childhood, we could go join the residents in their defense of the city," he cracked.

"No, thank you. I prefer it here."

"May I join you?"

"Of course," she said, patting the ledge beside her.

It was a short sample size to go on, given they had just reconnected, but he sounded more comfortable, not only with her but with himself—not always the case in the latter days of their previous courtship.

Dressed in the simplest of outfits—a tight, white t-shirt and jeans—he nonetheless appeared much the fashion figure, causing her to recall the balancing act she had committed to at the start of the day---to simultaneously engage him while maintaining a proper distance.

"Has it always been one of your goals to live by a large body of water or just this particular one?" she asked.

"Actually, I was more of a river guy, until I realized I was more suited to the sea."

"How so?"

"We're told by the scientists that time is like a river. You can sit on its bank and never touch it twice before the flow passes you by. It's the same with love, I learned several years back. Once it passes you by, it's gone, never to be recovered. On the other hand, the sea offers second chances. There is a permanence about it. If I can find here what once passed me by, I intend to hold onto it forever."

And here she thought she was the seeker, hanging around town waiting for him to make an appearance, when all along he was the one waiting for her to reappear. She looked to the sky. Right about now she wouldn't mind trading places with one of those half dozen hawks circling a cumulus cloud billowing upward from the warm waters. They were riding the thermals at hundred-yard intervals, holding to their positions as they took turns penetrating the thick white mass one after the other in an ethereal game of hide and seek, before reappearing moments later in the deep blue yonder. *At least the hawks are having fun*, she ruminated, *unlike the two ledge sitters lost in thought far below them.*

"How about a short walk on the beach?" he asked.

"I'm game," she responded, bearing in mind her rules of engagement for the day.

They slipped off their shoes and tread down a steep slope toward the shore to begin their trek. Except for a trio of boys surfing the restless waves, they had the beach to themselves. Tamra consciously folded her arms as though experiencing a chill in the air. She would keep them that way for the duration of the stroll, leery her ex-boyfriend, whether deliberately or out of habit, would take her by the hand, as he had done countless times in the past during one of their casual walks around town. Lending a hand to her distancing effort was the continuous clamor of the wind and waves, punctuated by the calls of the shorebirds, which smothered any attempt at meaningful conversation between the two. All for the better, she thought.

They returned to the ledge, ostensibly no more invigorated or relaxed than when they began.

"What happened between us, Tamra?" he boldly asked, breaking a brief silence.

Nothing happened, Wade...that was the problem, she was about to say, but didn't. "We moved on with our lives," she said instead.

"That's boiling it down to the basics. It's like saying history is nothing more than something happening followed by something else happening. What you mean is you moved on with your life. That's what happened."

The first barb of the day had been thrown. As sure as the waves washing ashore, she knew there would be more to come. The veneer of an amicable breakup was about to come off. He wasn't going to let this opportunity go by without setting things straight.

"Remember when you were living with your grandmother down in Seminole Heights?" he asked in a soother tone.

"Of course, I remember. We were dating at the time, were we not?" she answered, snapping off a barb of her own, despite his mellower approach,

"Yes, but it's the part after we stopped seeing each other that sticks with me. I have since come to realize what a mistake I had made in giving up on you so quickly…"

"Giving up on me? Didn't he just state I was the one who did the giving up?"

"…By then I knew you had moved on with your life. Unfortunately, I could not as easily move on with mine. As the old adage goes, you don't realize how much a person means to you until they're gone from your life. That being said…I refuse to believe that once you've found that special person and for whatever reason lose them, they are lost to you forever."

"You make it sound like a missing-person case, Wade. What was missing wasn't the person, it was the passion."

"If it was the passion that went missing, Tamra, then it was once there—was it not?"

She shook her head, refusing to acknowledge the truth of it.

"At minimum, I needed to be close by you, near enough to feel your presence, so I took the step of renting an apartment down the street from you---a second home, if you will. It was a fourth-floor unit with a direct view of your grandmother's residence. I subsequently spent many a day observing your comings and goings, while catching up on my legal work. Your non-workday routine was a simple one…grocery shopping on Saturday mornings…church on Sunday with your grandmother…an occasional date…Friday night outings with your girlfriends…all standard stuff…until the passing of your grandmother. I suspected something was up when she suddenly was no longer to be seen. I checked the obituaries and noted her passing. The next thing I knew your house was up for sale." Carson paused, as if woken by what could be going through her mind. "In case you're thinking this is stalking…"

"What else could you call it?" she sharply interjected.

"...Nosey neighbor syndrome. The fact is I never followed you, harassed you, called you, or threatened you in any way, nor would I ever. In other words, I never met the definition of stalker, which is the reason I decided not to trail after you once you sold your home and moved elsewhere. Not that I wasn't tempted to. It was just that the lawyer in me was telling me I would be crossing a line."

"Following the legal guidelines rather than the ethical ones, it appears to me, Wade."

Carson ignored her response and continued with his storyline. "My social life entered a new phase during this period. The law firm I now work for assigned me to what they term the borderline accounts...the crime syndicate clients who operate within the gray areas of the laws governing everything from illegal drug activity to bookmaking, prostitution, and gambling. I learned early on how important it was for these clients to be able to conduct their business in a seemingly above-board glamorous setting, a place even the politicians and law enforcement officials would have no problem patronizing."

A spray of water from a crashing wave reached their perch, pausing their conversation. An unsettled air permeated the Gulf atmosphere, as raucous calls of shorebirds, stirred into an airborne frenzy by the gusts of wind, filled the heavens. Dark gray matter began to coat the underbellies of the gathering clouds. Steadily, the darkness spread upward through the formations, giving birth to towering thunderheads.

Carson continued. "The goal of the mob bosses was to hook the officials to the lifestyle to the degree they would oppose any efforts to undermine the operations."

"And your job was to make it all appear legal," Tamra suggested, wondering where all this backstory of his was headed. She was coming to believe he had planned this day out on short notice and intended to execute it precisely as he drew it up. Why waste an opportunity, he seemed to have decided, now that they had unexpectedly crossed paths?

"The gambling and entertainment meccas have become the workplace of my professional life for the last six years. You might ask what all this has to do with you, so I will tell you. On day one of my assignment, I was introduced to a whole new category of women...beautiful women...street-smart women...willing women, mostly wannabes who had no qualms about trading favors for favors, all in the interest of climbing social and corporate ladders. Yeah, I learned a lot about women during that period, like when they tell you they prefer nice guys when they really don't. The truth is they like the cocky ones. They fit right into their preferred lifestyles."

Wade had gained a confidence alright, she noted. Must have come from working the floor at all those social functions he was required to attend as part of his job. She didn't know what to make of it. He was acting as if the prize he was after was already his, as though it was destined for him.

"In the beginning I considered it a welcome distraction from the obsession I had with you," he continued. "'An obsessive love disorder' is how a therapist I ended up seeing described it. 'There are three stages to the condition,' he patiently explained to me—monitoring, controlling, and possessing.' I told him I had never made it past the first one. Then he pointed out something interesting. It had to do with the old saying 'love possessed is love lost.' It seems the first two stages are not always necessary when the third is right there for the asking. Besides, you really don't know whether it was love or lust all along, until the relationship is consummated. Only then will the truth come out. The point is, why dwell on the first two stages when you can bypass them with the third."

"Right there for the asking?"

"His words."

"Based on your input. You did say the therapist was a male—right?" Tamra asked with a trace of sarcasm.

"Yes...why? Are you thinking there's no truth to the adage?"

"There may be general truth to the adage, but love and obsession are two conditions I don't normally associate with each other, Wade," she pointedly said, wary of any past subliminal chemistry between the two that might be reawakened.

"Well, apparently it was in that guy's catalog of conditions and recommended cures for them."

"Shortcuts to take rather than cures, it sounds to me."

"Hey, whatever works was my mindset at the time, and since nothing seemed to be working, I decided to go in a different direction by settling for a woman far less challenging than you."

"In what way?"

"In every way."

In Tamra's mind the confessions of Wade Carson were less a religious testament than a woe-is-me screed. If given the power, she would gladly grant him absolution from his secular sin of excessive lusting and be done with him. Alas, that was not an option considering she had a client to serve. The conundrum she faced was a straightforward one. Wade wanted badly to get her into his bed, whereas she needed to get into his house to verify if his abused wife was presently residing there. The solution to the predicament came from the heavens in the form of a loud rumble of thunder. "We're about to get rained on," he said, rising to his feet and extending a helping hand. "Come on, I'll show you the house." She took it, but deftly released it once to her feet.

They walked up Seacrest Street, the avenue bordering the seawall, as the first droplets of rain fell randomly along their path. They passed a row of homes mega-buck lottery winners might find affordable, Tamra noted. Halfway up the street, they came upon a two-story wood-framed house colored a pastel gray.

"This is it," he said, guiding her up to the front entrance.

"How long have you owned this place?"

"I don't own it. It's a rental."

He opened the front door and motioned her in with a wave of the hand.

"Is your wife home?" she asked upon entering.

"Does it matter?" he answered back, rousing her unease.

The interior of the home had a pronounced masculine flavor to it. Terra-cotta colored walls framed a hard, oaken floor upon which were scattered various pieces of dark mahogany furniture. The flavor of the room extended to the atmospherics. Tamra could have sworn there was a musk-scented air freshener operating behind the scene.

"Have a seat," he said, lowering himself into a large sofa. She, in turn, chose an armchair facing him from across the room. "Normally, we leave the windows open and the air off this time of the year so we can enjoy the sea breezes," he said. "However, with the storm bearing down, I shut them before I left. Is it comfortable enough for you? I could turn on the air if you like."

"Don't bother...I'm fine."

"Care for a drink?"

"No, thank you."

"So, tell me, what does your fiancé do for a living?"

"He's a private investigator."

The revelation drew a surprised look from her host. "Interesting...I would have guessed him to be a doctor, banker, hedge fund manager, venture capitalist, even an attorney---someone along those lines---a professional for sure."

She ignored the dig, though her pique must have been written on her face.

"Not that private eyes are not professional. I simply view them as the blue-collar class of the legal field. Any reason he didn't accompany you on your trip here?"

"He's working on an out-of-town case."

"Which town?"

"Kansas City for one."

"Nice city...I've been there on a couple of occasions. When's the marriage?"

"We haven't set a final date," she fibbed, for no good reason other than a voice inside her told her to. "Sometime soon."

"This calls for a special wedding gift...special enough to honor the occasion...something that can't be re-gifted. Not that you would do that," he added with a grin. "I'll see what I can come up with. By the way, I like your sundress. You should wear them more often—or maybe you do. They certainly highlight your attributes, as if they needed highlighting. You always had a way of finding that sweet spot between the knee and the thigh to land the hems of those dresses of yours," he continued. "I call it the demarcation line between the cheesy and the classy."

His observation drew no comment from her, though she did have to fight off the impulse to smooth her dress. No question, he was now oozing confidence, which was not only palpable but for her a danger as well. There's a reason that confident men, more times than not, get what they want. They boast a winning record and who isn't drawn to a winner, whatever their pursuit?

"Sorry," he said, reading her. "I intended it as a compliment."

"No problem. I'll take it as one."

Yes, there was something very different about Wade Carson from the man she once knew, the guy with whom she had a relationship that never advanced much beyond a goodnight kiss. No longer were his eyes the plain, passionless orbs he continually had on display. Somehow, they had become harbingers of his many mood swings, appearing from one moment to the next—indifferent, engaging, hypnotic, and surprisingly sensual. Why the change in him? Perhaps it was the walk on the wild side he had taken in the long interim since she had last seen him. Whatever, she found it all unsettling. In this house, in his presence, in an increasingly sultry, charged atmosphere, she had become disturbingly conscious of her sexuality.

Stepped right into the wolf's lair, didn't you Tamra?

The raindrops pelting the roof grew more intense. The skies outside had darkened further, in turn dimming the ambient light in the room, rendering it to shadows.

"Do you recall the day we both confessed to being pluviophiles---lovers of rain?" he asked through the dimness.

"I do, though at the time I was completely ignorant of the term for it."

If she was to pick the best time they had together, it would be the one he was referring to. It was the day they spent on the barrier island of Siesta Key, sitting on a lanai, listening to the soft pitter patter of an all-day rain on the tin roof and broad leaves of several sea-grape trees clustered in the backyard like a mini rainforest. The home belonged to a friend of his who invited them to spend the day there while he and his wife were off on a day trip to the Everglades.

The rain that day may have spoiled an intended beach outing but in return offered an incredibly relaxed setting...perfect for a couple of self-professed pluviophiles. Two cushioned wicker chairs, a bottle of wine, a stocked fridge, a functioning outdoor grill, reggae music on the stereo, and a volunteer cook in Wade was all that was needed to make life good that day on Siesta Key. The two had found common ground in their eagerness to live in the moment. The rain does that...turns up the empathy and intensifies it, allowing you and your companion in an earthy, quiet, personal way to connect on a basic human level, often without uttering a word. On such an occasion, the feelings toward another intensify. Now that she looked back on it, what was not to like? If not for the early arrival back home of the homeowner, it might have been the first time her relationship with Wade advanced beyond a goodnight kiss.

Presently, she could sense her ex-boyfriend gazing at her from across the room. Clearly, he was in tune with her recollection of their experience together on Siesta Key and the incompleteness of it. Was this his effort to recapture the moment? And where was his wife? she was about to ask him, but didn't. For fear of what? That it might disrupt their twisted reunion dance?

"If you want something bad enough, you're going to get it, Tamra," he said, throwing another old axiom her way. "Another thing I learned while traveling the fast lane...women like to be desired...the good ones as well as the bad ones. It's a universal truth. They can sense the desire in a man like a wild animal senses the fear in a prey. The sole difference is they don't have to go on the attack to devour it. Sooner or later, it will come to them."

He was right. Women like to be desired, including her, and when a man carries an all-consuming passion for someone, as he clearly does for her, it's not something easily discounted given the right circumstances. If he feels this strongly about her, should his passion not be rewarded, particularly when there's a reasonable chance it would rid him of his obsession? All it would require is a single intimate episode of her letting him have his way.

You live in the moment...

She knew what was coming next, as she glimpsed him through the shadows leaving the couch to casually approach her from across the room, becoming more visible with each step. He came to a stop within an arm's reach of her, at which point he extended his hand for her to take. Emotions churning and defenses weakening, she looked past his hand deep into his eyes and then deeper behind them, wherein she found her answer.

"No."

Slowly, he lowered his hand. "What can he offer you, Tamra, that I can't? More love? More passion? I don't think so, nor do I think you think so."

Tamra's senses jolted to reality. *What makes him think I can be so fickle as to trade my fiancé for a romantic encounter with a philandering lawyer working for the Mafiosa?*

"You think wrong, Wade. I'll tell you exactly what he can offer me that you never could—trust and loyalty. I trust him in everything he does and everything he says, especially each and every time he tells me he loves me."

A low, long roll of thunder shook the house, followed closely by the creak of a door opening above them. On a second-floor walkway appeared a woman dressed in a flowing white nightgown, looking much like a figure straight out of a Gothic tale. Tamra at once recognized her from the picture her brother had provided her. The presence of his wife, however, did nothing to cool the ardor of Tamra's would-be seducer, as he continued to keep his eyes fixated on her. Meanwhile, his wife stepped to the walkway railing and with an expressionless face looked down upon the scene as though it was as normal as the incoming and outgoing tides. Outgoing is where she needed to be, Tamra decided, grabbing her handbag and bolting toward the front door and through it, leaving her naked to the storm. She hustled down the front walk to the street, breaking into a trot once she reached it. The humid air was thick with the earthy scent of sodded flowers and shrubs. Moments later, having borne the brunt of the wind and rain, she was sitting in her car at the edge of the seawall, contemplating what had happened. "What was I thinking?" she asked aloud, knowing full well the answer was buried in the question. She wasn't thinking, certainly not with her head. A shiver went through her, followed closely by a rush of guilt that overcame her like a surging wave through a breached seawall.

Get control of yourself. You got what you came for, now finish the job!

She exhaled a deep breath, ignited the engine, and headed back to the motel.

———

BACK IN HER ROOM, she wasted no time contacting Mickey Riley to let him know she had located his sister and brother-in-law in Boca Grande.

"Is she there as we speak?" he asked.

"As of this morning, she was there. They're renting a home."

"What's the address?"

Wouldn't you know it. Amid all the excitement, she had forgotten a basic step. "Stupid me...I failed to jot it down. However, I can tell you it's the sixth house up from the south end of Seacrest Street, which is where the seawall is located and the street begins. It will be on your left-hand side as you travel north on it. The home is a two-story, wood-framed residence, painted a pale gray color. Carson's car is parked in the driveway. It's a blue Lexus."

"Yep, I've seen it before," he said. "Good work, Tamra. I'm on my way down as soon as I hang up."

She next dialed Adam at home and the office. Still no answer. She wanted to remind him it was past time to get on board with the cell phone technology once these cases were closed, that they were way behind on it. Not an easy thing to do when dealing with a man...a relatively young one at that...who constantly made known his preference for the old ways, from fountain pens to crank phones. If he had it his way, it would be a forties-style P.I. office, from furnishings to clothing. Yes, it was frustrating, though the thought of it brought a much-needed smile to her face.

She estimated it would take Riley about one and a half to two hours at the most to reach Boca Grande. That would give her plenty of time to take a relaxing shower and still make it to Seacrest Street before his arrival. Until she witnessed Susan Carson leaving the property with her brother, she would not consider the case closed.

She took the shower and threw on a pair of jeans and a tank top. Moments later, she was steering her Jeep through banyan-canopied streets toward Seacrest. On arriving, she parked her car at the north end of the avenue, close enough for her to witness the upcoming proceedings. She had barely settled in when a white SUV entered the street from the south end, pulling to a stop across from the Carson rental. Riley at once hopped out of the vehicle, jogged across the road and up the front sidewalk to the front door. He pounded on it with his fist, deciding to forego the doorbell. Tamra had considered alerting the sheriff's station on the island to the potential of a domestic disturbance but decided the chance for violence was remote. It would be foolish for Carson to instigate a physical confrontation with a stoked, much larger man. After all, he had a public reputation to uphold, fake as it was. A violent altercation could end up exposing the shady undertakings of the organization he represented, should the media ever get wind of it. No doubt his mob bosses would not take kindly to anyone on the payroll drawing unnecessary attention from law enforcement officials, particularly when it was his job to keep them at bay.

It took a second pounding from Riley for Carson to open the door. The two appeared to exchange words, at which point Carson retreated back into the house, closing the door behind him.

Riley paced in front of the entrance for several minutes, before the door reopened. Out stepped his sister whom he at once took by the arm and led to his car. As the drama unfolded, a movement at a second-floor window caught Tamra's eye. Wade Carson was staring down at the scene below, not at his wife and brother-in-law, but at the woman sitting in the Jeep parked up the street.

They're usually about some demented guy's passion to control another. The moment you show up, you become a threat to take away that control.

Adam's words hung in the back of her mind. Up till now, she was convinced Carson was blind to her mission to locate his wife. They were simply two old flames who happened to cross paths, much to each other's delight, though for very different reasons. Sure, his suspicion probably was tweaked when she let it be known her betrothed was a private investigator. Yet, he was so focused on her, he ostensibly considered it little more than a temporary distraction. The appearance of his wife's brother on his doorstep, however, lifted the wool from his eyes. He had been betrayed and by a woman who had a front row seat to observe her handiwork.

Once Riley drove away, Tamra ignited the Jeep's engine, made a slow U-turn, and returned to the motel.

———

SHE COULD HAVE PACKED up and left the island at that point but chose otherwise. She had already paid for another night and was not about to turn tail on the chance Carson might seek retribution for what he no doubt felt was a deliberate humiliation. He could as easily find her in Tampa as he could Boca Grande. If she was to handle future cases on the street with a high degree of confidence, she could not be worrying about potential blowback from them— or him in particular.

In a move toward normalcy, she elected to spend the evening at one of her favorite beach-side restaurants south of town. Following a short coastal drive, she was sitting at an outdoor table enjoying a grouper sandwich and iced tea. Remnants of the morning storm had dissipated, leaving behind serene waters and a light surf brushing the shoreline.

She lingered through the quiet of the sunset, letting it ease her mind from the disquiet of the day. Her thoughts eventually drifted to the question of what life would be like living full time in Boca Grande when who should enter the scene—none other than Wade Carson, accompanied by a willowy redhead dressed in a yellow sundress. They took a table two rows in front of her. As soon as they were seated, her ex-boyfriend cast a quick glance back her way and acknowledged her presence with a weak smile and a nod, before leaning over to whisper a few words to his lady friend.

Happenstance? No way, Tamra mused—more like a bad ruse to get into her head. She had been prepared to leave when the two made their appearance. Now she decided to settle in a while longer. She was not going to give him the satisfaction of seeing her appear to cut and run. She ordered another iced tea and to ease her mind recalled the trajectory of her life that eventually led to this point.

———

Born and bred in the small railroad town of Altoona, Pennsylvania, she was the daughter of a mine worker. Unfortunately, tragedy struck her at the early age of five when her father was killed in a mining accident. All she could vaguely remember of the episode was her mother disappearing soon after. As related to her later by her nana, her mother turned to the bottle to drown her sorrows. She also had no financial support to speak of and with her life spinning out of control, she decided to give her daughter up to her mother to raise. For a five-year-old it was too much to absorb, much less understand. Not long after she moved in with her grandmother, her mother ran off with a newfound boyfriend. A "ne'er-do-well" her nana called him. They were never to be heard from again. If not for her grandmother taking her under her wing, who knows where she might have landed. A ward of the state? A stable guardian she needed and a stable guardian she got. She could not have asked for a better childhood than the one she spent under her nana's tutelage.

Her favorite remembrances were those surrounding the small garment shop her grandmother, along with two of her friends, operated out of the basement of their home. They made it a success by concentrating primarily on a niche market—uniforms for parochial school students, cheerleading squads, and restaurant workers. As a young girl, she took a great interest in the business, spending many hours in the basement shop watching the seamstresses going about their work—cutting patterns, selecting thread colors, operating the sewing machines, measuring customers and fabric. She particularly enjoyed the creative aspects of the trade. During one stage of the operation, her grandmother came up with the idea of making a child's apron with pockets lining the front into which the kids could stash their crayons and whatever without making a mess of things. The exciting part for her came when her nana chose her to do the modeling of the item in an advertisement. They planned to run it in a trade magazine. It was the first of her many modeling experiences with the business.

Through grade school and high school, the garment shop became a big part of her life, so much so she considered asking her grandmother if she could one day take over the business. It was not to be, however. Following her high school graduation, her grandmother decided to shut down the operation and retire to Florida, taking her granddaughter along with her. "There's no future for you here," she advised her. "You best come with me to Tampa." She did, and for the first few years, divided her time between attending the local community college, where she was pursuing an associate degree in criminal justice, and part-time secretarial jobs. Upon completing her degree, she went looking for a full-time position that would provide her an entry into her field of study. It was then she saw the ad for a position at Adam Fraley's Private Investigations.

A soft smile curled her lips as she recalled their first meeting. She was the applicant, he the interviewer. The position up for grabs was that of office manager, Adam's previous job, before he took over Pete Peterson's Private Investigations business. You would have thought she'd be the nervous one, he the experienced professional. As she learned later, it was the first job interview he had ever conducted. To this day it remains so.

When she asked him after the original interview how many he planned on conducting, he said one and hired her. "It's a tradition around here. It's the same way my old boss hired me," he said. At the time, she didn't know whether to take that as a compliment or not. Whatever the reason for the quick action, it was the first of what she considered the mile markers in their relationship.

The second marker was the first case she was assigned to, one that temporarily took her from behind the desk into the field while Adam held down the office. It turned out to be a near debacle. She was asked by Adam to play a decoy in a dangerous ploy to lure an alleged killer cop he was tailing into divulging information that would solidify the case against him. Instead, it almost got her killed, resulting in a heart-felt apology from her boss and a promise it would never happen again. Still, it was a marker in that it signaled she was no longer confined exclusively to desk duty.

The third was the decision by Adam to cross the personal-professional divide by asking her out on a date, something she never encouraged but welcomed. She knew the whole office romance issue was a contentious one in business circles, particularly when it involved a supervisor-subordinate situation. The fact it occurred in a two-person, small business setting where collateral damage was unlikely to occur eased their minds as to the propriety of it. Of course, that was true only if the relationship endured. The wisdom of it aside, she was always of the belief the workplace presented a good opportunity for getting to know someone. She had no idea what Preston Penrod's secret to achieving "consummate intimacy" entailed, though she had long ago come to her own belief that the truest intimacy between two people was the intimacy of thought, a prerequisite in her view toward physical intimacy. What better environment to get the process started than in the social interaction offered by the workplace where true selves are eventually exposed?

The fourth marker came as a complete surprise when Adam decided to start a family by adopting Noelle, an orphaned child he chanced upon while working a case in Colorado. It also led to a lifestyle change for her, as she in effect became the surrogate mother for the child, a role she had come to cherish.

The most recent marker came when Adam asked her to marry him and she accepted. In so doing, he set their little business on its present path to becoming a mom-and-pop operation.

———

A SUDDEN GUST of wind coming in off the Gulf interrupted Tamra's reminiscing. The burst of air spun table umbrellas, ruffled customers' hair, and sent loose items flying. The wind quickly subsided and normalcy returned to the restaurant, at which point her waitress walked over and handed her a note. "The gentleman in the jeans and blue shirt asked me to give you this." Tamra opened it and with a degree of trepidation read it.

It said "Rescue Me."

If not for the waitress pointing out who actually sent the message, she just as easily could have concluded it came from his redheaded companion.

She set aside the message and glanced her ex-boyfriend's way. *The guy sure knew how to ruin a gorgeous sunset.*

At the moment, he was looking past the redhead toward her. A thin, cocksure smile was pasted to his face. She had seen that smile before, right after he began that stroll across his living room floor to go one-on-one with her earlier that day.

And how exactly should she go about rescuing him? More to the point—why should she? To give him a second go at her by surrendering her life for the sake of his? No, she'd reserve that for family members. Rather than undertake a rescue mission she had no appetite for, she instead chose to remove herself from the scene immediately, before it reached cringe-worthy status. By all means she should do nothing to encourage him, though she may already have by simply hanging around after they arrived.

The sun had set and the last streaks of daylight were nearing their final fade to black, when she grabbed her purse, paid the waitress, and exited the scene with nary a glance back. By nightfall she was back in the motel room, preparing for an early bedtime. She tried contacting Adam with no luck. He apparently had yet to return from his trip. Satisfied she had accomplished all she could for the day, she slipped into bed and into a troubled sleep, one filled with disturbing, concupiscent images of what-might-have-been in her close encounter with her former boyfriend.

Abruptly, she was wakened, not by the nightmarish images, but instead by a flood of bright light from someone's high beams streaming through the sheer window curtains directly facing her bed. All of a sudden, the room was transformed into a ghostly white. She glanced at a digital clock radio on a bedside stand. It was midnight. She tossed aside the covers, sat on the edge of the bed, and squinted at the light. She waited...and waited...for the lights to go out as more troubling images reentered her mind. Was he here for another attempt? She debated whether to step outside and tell the driver to douse his lights or call the desk clerk to complain. She did neither. Her patience was finally rewarded when she heard a woman call out from the parking area, "Honey, you forgot to turn off the lights."

After another round of tossing and turning, she went back to sleep, only to be reawakened again with a start—this time by an early morning wake-up call she forgot she had requested the previous day.

She dressed and gathered her belongings, throwing them into the back of her Jeep. She then walked to the office to check out. On the way back to her car, she spotted a handwritten note attached to the door of the room she had just vacated. She snatched it, held it under a walkway light, and read the contents.

"Five minutes of your time...that's all I ask."

The specter she had expected overnight had arrived. She glanced over her shoulder to survey the grounds. The centerpiece of the motel complex was a compact courtyard ringed by several wooden benches and canopied by a mid-sized banyan tree. There was enough ambient light in the pre-dawn hour for her to identify the figure sitting on one of the benches. By all measures of rational reasoning, she should have ignored his presence and left. Why she didn't defied explanation. Instead, she acquiesced to his request and walked to where he sat, his attention ostensibly tuned to his inner thoughts.

"Wade...what are you doing here?" she asked directly on her approach.

He was wearing the same garb he had worn at the beach

restaurant the previous evening. Bedraggled and disheveled, he had the look of an unmade bed. Weariness clouded his eyes.

"I came to talk to you," he said, slowly turning his attention to her.

"Wade, I..."

He held up his hand and with the other, patted the bench, inviting her to join him.

"What is it you want?" she asked, taking a seat a decent distance from him, yet close enough to catch a whiff of alcohol. "I don't have much time."

"Remember that first night I met you, when I asked your girlfriend, all in fun of course, to introduce me to you, and that if she didn't, it would be the worst thing that would ever happen to me in my life? Well, it turns out the opposite is true. If she hadn't introduced me, I'd probably be a much happier man right about now."

"Yet, you're here to see me," she replied, her patience already wearing thin in this second go-around. "You seemed to be having a good time with your girlfriend last evening. That should have lasted you at least for the remainder of the weekend."

"My girlfriend," he said with a hearty chuckle. "I'll have you know she's a member of the world's oldest profession, one of the island's finest call girls. She can empty a wallet faster than a card shark."

"What is it you want to say to me, Wade?" she asked in frustration.

"Oh, I don't know. I was hoping you had something to say to me, now that the storm has passed," he said, rubbing his face with his hands. "If only the one in my head would follow it."

"I can't help you with that, Wade."

"Sure, you can. You already have with your presence. Can't you see?"

She had no choice but to cut off the conversation before it became never-ending. Five minutes would turn to ten, ten to twenty, and twenty to sixty with no end in sight. And for what? To simply satisfy that female altruistic streak in her? No, she wasn't going to wait around for the "I-can't-live-without-you" line. If she had had any sense, she would have left immediately after reading his note. The reality was he was going to have to live his life without her, whether he realized it or not. She was not about to become another in the string of what he deemed cold women in his life. She rose from the bench. "I'm going home," she said, and walked to her car. A short while later, she was crossing the causeway, on her way off the island just as dawn was breaking. Alas, the glorious sunrise was not the lasting image she would take from the island. Instead, it was the image of Wade Carson slouched on that motel bench, specifically the pitiful cast to his face. Whether it was on a sick pet of hers or a self-destructing former boyfriend, the pitiful look grabbed hold of her every time with little sign of letting go.

———

DURING THE DRIVE HOME, the revelation by her ex-boyfriend that he had staked out her grandmother's house gnawed at her. Of all his indiscretions, this one troubled her most. It was one thing to violate her privacy, but to trespass on her grandmother's took his recklessness to another level. What really rankled her was the realization that she herself was partly to blame, having taken up with the guy in the first place.

With the memory of her grandmother weighing heavily on her mind, she decided to pay a visit to her nana's final resting place in Highland Cemetery, stopping along the way to pick up a bouquet of flowers. It was a relatively new burial site that appeared by design less a graveyard than a vast green landscape dotted by live oak trees and an occasional gravesite. Considered one of the first eco-friendly cemeteries, it featured a creek meandering through it. Take away the grave markers and from a distance it resembled a layout for a golf course or public park.

She passed through the opened cast iron gate and eased her Jeep along a gravel road to the foot of a pedestrian path that wound its way over grounds carpeted by freshly cut Bermuda grass. The pathway led up a gentle rise at the top of which stood a tall oak tree, its crooked limbs clearly visible against the backdrop of a clear blue sky. "Bury me next to an oak tree," her grandmother would often say and thus Tamra did.

She snatched the bouquet from the passenger seat and began the trek to the top of the rise, the sounds of birdsong and rustling wind accompanying her along the way. Halfway up she noticed something strange and new on the landscape. Her grandmother was no longer alone. Aside her plot appeared another gravesite, unusual in that only family members are normally entombed in such close proximity to each other. The reason for it became clear the moment she stepped in front of the headstone and read the inscription on it.

Elaine Fugit
Beloved daughter
July, 1937-March, 1996

Tamra caught her breath and at once put her mind in rewind as the questions rushed forth. Why wasn't she told? Her grandmother must have prearranged the burial. Was her mother living here all this time? If so, she surely would have tried to contact her daughter, one would think. Through the years she had occasionally queried her grandmother as to whether her mother was still alive. Invariably, she would reply "Leave her be, honey. All you need to know is she loves you." In the present tense, she would say it, as though she was still in regular contact with her.

Lying at the base of her mother's headstone was a withered bouquet of sunflowers, tweaking her curiosity as to who may have left them. Was she destined to go through the remainder of her life not knowing whether there were siblings of hers out there roaming the world? Perhaps one day a sister or brother will come looking for her.

Prodded by the thought, she looked about her, imagining such an occasion. What if the sibling should unexpectedly walk up at this very moment intending to pay respect to their mother? How awkward would that be—the two of them standing here—strangers —each waiting for the other to ask "Why are you here?" Then again, it was only awkward if you allowed it to be so. The cure for such a moment, she had learned from past experience, is finding common ground to stand on, and what could be more common for them than this ground?

The truth was it would not be difficult for her to apply her investigative skills to uncover the mystery of her mother's last fifty or so years. Of that she was certain. And who better to do it? She could start the process right this moment by walking over to the cemetery office and asking a few pertinent questions. If need be, she could opt for clandestine surveillance tactics. It wasn't not like they were unusual in cemetery settings. She was aware of how front gate locks could be picked overnight to plant hidden microphones and cameras a few feet from gravesites to monitor visitors or nab vandals. She once was told by a veteran P.I. that cemetery officials occasionally would resort to conducting sweeps of the grounds to unearth devices surreptitiously placed by outside entities. Yet, the overriding question hung there---in doing so, would she be dishonoring her nana's wishes and those of her mother?

She gathered her thoughts and weighed them, while at the same time attempting to resurrect the blurred image of a mother missing from her life all these years. Try as she might to conjure up a vision of her, she was unable to do so. Old photos of her mother were nonexistent, either cast away or never taken. At one stage she turned to a therapist to help her overcome her childhood amnesia. The regimen the therapist recommended ran the gamut of memory-inducing triggers, from reading old newspaper clippings and scrapbooks, to speaking with former neighbors and relatives. The advice also came with a warning from the therapist: "Digging up the past sometimes serves no good purpose, so beware of creating false memories. It's easy to do when one's focus and desire are intense enough to see things that aren't there." In the end, the results were deeply disappointing and she essentially gave up the effort.

Through the long stretch of intervening years, she frequently dwelled on the three things she ultimately decided she would say to her mother should they ever be reunited. Sadly, as of today, it had become a moot point. Still, who's to say a mother's intuition isn't strong enough to reach beyond the grave? With that in mind, she took the bouquet of flowers and divided it into two, placing one half at the foot of her grandmother's headstone before stepping over to her mother's gravesite to lay the remaining half.

"Thank you, Mother, for giving me life. If it's forgiveness you want, I forgive you. If it's my love you want, you'll have it always."

She took a step back to take a final look at the two gravesites. "Rest in peace," she whispered, leaving undisturbed the memories of both women buried forever in her mind.

CHAPTER NINE

ON HIS RETURN HOME FROM THE TAMPA AIRPORT, ADAM OPTED to swing by the former rental home of Manny and Timmy for no better reason than to ponder where he might have gone wrong from the beginning of the case. Or perhaps it was just a loose end he felt needed to be tied up to put a capper on it. Approaching the home, he noticed someone had taken the trouble to clean up the lawn and place a "For Rent" sign out front. Attached to the sign was a pamphlet holder. He parked his car and jumped out to retrieve one of the handouts. It gave the phone number and business address of the rental agent who went by the name of George Yearling. He recognized the address as an office plaza located a short drive away and decided to pay Mr. Yearling an unannounced visit.

———

GEORGE YEARLING WAS A MIDDLE-AGED, ruddy-faced man with balding head rimmed by dyed brown hair hanging to the collar of his yellow flannel shirt. His office had a sterile, government look to it, marked by gray metal chairs and desk. The drab olive-colored walls, ceiling, and floor added to the dingy ambience.

"Have a chair," he said to his visitor in a smoker's voice. "What can I do for you?"

Adam threw his story out there, having no sense of whether it would land on receptive ears or not. To his surprise Mr. Yearling was more prepared to engage him on the topic than he expected.

"Yeah, Manny and Timmy were not the best of renters. Young tenants in general have a way of not maintaining a home, I'm sad to say. I suppose they're too accustomed to having their parents around to pick up after them. Nevertheless, they both signed the rental agreement, which called for them to keep up the property, so they really have no case against the eviction. Business is business, whether it's the government or the private sector that's involved."

"They kept up with their rent payments?"

"Yep, no issue there. Manny came from a wealthy South American family. Money was no problem for him."

"And Timmy? What was the source of his income?"

"Manny was the source of his income, or to be precise--- Manny's parents. Timmy's family is–lower middle class. If I recall right, they have five kids to support."

Yearling's phone rang, interrupting the exchange. He quickly ended it, telling the caller he was busy at the moment. Meanwhile, Adam was welcoming the fact the guy was entirely open with him. "Yet, he paid his share of the rent on time?" he asked.

"It was paid by Manny. They had a joint checking account, though there was no question in my mind where the funds were coming from."

"How did that happen...a joint checking account? Have any idea?"

"It shows the relationship that developed between the two."

"In what way?"

"I was around them enough to listen and observe their interaction. It wasn't unusual for them to invite me to hang around for a beer after one of my periodic inspections to see how things were going. I was sure it was a ploy on their part to keep them in my good graces despite the demerits I was pointing out to them. It was clear Timmy controlled the relationship. He was continually dominating and exploiting his housemate. He was sort of a—what do you call it? Svingaly?"

"Svengali."

"Yeah, more like a frat house Svengali, if there is such a thing."

"What about their schooling?"

The landlord let out a hearty guffaw. "School was secondary to them, more so Timmy. I never saw the guy once crack a book."

"Did Manny run a messaging service from home at one time?" Adam asked.

The question drew another laugh. "That was Timmy's cockamamie idea that never saw the light of day. He was always coming up with get-rich schemes."

"Timmy's exploitation of Manny extended to financial matters?"

"You bet, especially when it came to their travels. He wasn't just riding the Manny gravy train. He was driving it. He could hardly let a weekend go by without a trip to Las Vegas."

"It was Timmy who couldn't let one go by?" Adam asked with surprise in his eyes.

"Yes, Timmy. He was always enamored with the Vegas lifestyle. He would usually take Manny along with him—less for his companionship than his financial input, I'm sure. I don't think Manny had an appreciation of how much money they were spending, having come from a family that would probably consider it small change. I'm a former gambler myself," Yearling confessed. "I was one step away from becoming a compulsive one after becoming addicted to the one-armed bandits. In my case it turned out to be more than an addiction. It became a necessity. Even when I won, I was not jumping for joy. My sole thought was to win more. Of course, it's never enough. It doesn't matter whether you're young or old to become addicted. No one is immune to the fever, especially if you live in proximity to the gaming centers, which I did at the time. Today, that isn't even a factor with the arrival of online gambling. It's like any other high-demand product. Eventually, it will be delivered straight to your doorstep."

"What was your biggest payday?" Adam asked out of curiosity.

Yearling did not hesitate with his answer. "My biggest payday was the day I decided not to play. That's the day you realize you're on the road to recovery."

"Back to Timmy...are you saying he accompanied Manny on their most recent trip to Vegas?"

"He sure did. They gave me a heads-up they were going. That's the first thing I found surprising about your story—that Manny went alone and was being chased by mob guys because of gambling debts. The second thing was that Timmy told you Manny had been gone for about four months. No, way. He's been gone less than a week and that was to Vegas with Timmy."

Adam tried to make sense of this. After all, he had talked to Timmy at the rental house. And Manny was on the bus heading to Kansas City—without Timmy—which he knew from firsthand observation.

"Why did Manny take the bus home and why wasn't Timmy with him?"

"Manny always took the bus for the most basic of reasons...he had a deep fear of flying. Hell, he didn't even fly here from Colombia when he first started school. He took a boat to Miami and then a bus here."

"So, Timmy arrived home first from Vegas and apparently no one was chasing him. I guess Manny was the chosen one, the weakest of their prey, or the one with the money ties."

"Or they just lost track of Timmy. That kid is slippery in more ways than one," Yearling said. "I could see him skipping out on Manny."

"Somehow he must have learned Manny was being tailed. It could have been that Manny contacted him by phone at the Vegas airport to let him know."

"Which led Timmy to get the hell out of there," Yearling said. "So much for lending a friend a helping hand."

"Letting me know Manny was being tailed and was riding a bus home were about the only things he told me that were true...that and the flow of funds regularly coming in from his parents." Adam said.

"What about Timmy? Have you tried to contact him?" Yearling asked.

"I don't know what good it would do. I'm certain he has no idea of where Manny is. Plus, he's not my client. I really have no interest in his welfare, especially after he flat-out lied to me."

"You're certain he has no idea?" Yearling asked through a sly smile, planting a seed of doubt in Adam's mind.

Adam shook his head. "I'm sure," he said, dismissing the thought.

Yearling reached for his desk phone and dialed a number. "He's back living with his parents in Sarasota. Why don't you ask him?" he said, handing him the phone.

Adam reluctantly took it. A woman was on the other end of the line answering the call. "Could I speak to Timmy," he asked.

"May I tell him who's calling?"

"An old friend," he said, figuring the kid might skip the call if he identified himself.

"Does the old friend have a name?" the woman asked derisively, leading Adam to believe Timmy may be a chip off the old block.

"Fred," he said, not really caring if the fake name prevented Timmy from coming to the phone.

"Hold on."

"Hello," came the subdued salutation a moment later.

Maybe he did know a Fred after all, Adam mused.

"Timmy, this is Adam Fraley, the private investigator you spoke to the other day. I'm calling about your friend Manny."

Timmy paused a moment before answering. "Did you find him?" the kid asked.

"No, I haven't. I was about to ask if you've heard from him."

"No."

"Why didn't you tell me you were in Las Vegas with him, Timmy?" he asked straight out.

"I never said I was," he answered hesitantly.

"Don't play games…"

"Sorry, I've got to run…hope you find him," he hurriedly said, before hanging up.

Yearling had a wry smile on his face as Adam handed him back the phone. "I told you the kid's slippery. A few experiences with him will make just about anyone appreciate their own upbringing. You going after him?"

"Nope. I'm convinced he's got no idea where Manny is, nor does he care. By the way, how old are those two…do you know?"

"I can find out for you…date of birth is asked for on the rental application."

Yearling played with the keys on his desk computer to call up the completed applications. "Let's see…Manny is twenty…and give me another second and I'll see how old Timmy is…he is twenty-two. Why do you ask?"

"The legal age for gambling in Nevada is twenty-one. They won't let anyone under that age into a casino. The gaming operators are strict in that regard."

"What does that tell you?" Yearling asked.

"Timmy told me Manny had sought out funds from an illegal operation because he was underage. It was a half-truth. More likely, Manny was sitting back in the hotel room while Timmy was out blowing away his parents' money."

"You were thinking at the time it was an illegal operation they were dealing with, yet it mattered how old they were?"

"Even the illegal mob operators have policies to abide by. Dealing with kids is likely among them. It's a moot point now. As you've documented, Timmy was no kid and certainly no angel. It might well have been him that put the goons on Manny's tail, just to get them off his."

Adam rose from his chair. "I have to get to my office. I thank you for your input."

"No problem. If those two had kept up the property, I may not have been so free with the information. Besides, I may be in need of a P.I. myself somewhere down the line."

Adam reached for his billfold, pulled out a business card and dropped it on the desk. "Call me, if and when that happens," he said and left for his office.

CHAPTER TEN

ADAM WAS SITTING AT HIS DESK, RECOUNTING THE EVENTS surrounding his journey up north and side trip to speak with George Yearling, when Tamra walked into the office and took a seat in a client chair across from him without saying a word.

"No hug?" he asked.

Both rose from their chairs, half-circled the desk, and exchanged a tight embrace...extra tight on her part, it felt to Adam.

"Well, did you find them?" he asked, as they reclaimed their chairs.

"Yes, I found them. Susan Carson is now back with her brother... Adam, I need to tell you something concerning the case."

"What is it?" he asked, noting the worry on her face.

"Not long after I took the case, I discovered that Susan Carson's husband happened to be a former boyfriend of mine. Despite that, I decided to continue with it."

Adam shrugged. "So?"

"There were obviously potential conflicts of interest, both professionally and personally," she answered, surprised at his indifference to her revelation.

"Listen...as my old boss Pete Peterson once told me, 'There are all sorts of potential conflicts of interest you're going to run into in this business...former girlfriends, former co-workers, former bosses, former classmates, former enemies, former spouses...the 'former' list is endless. 'At the end of the day, there are only two questions to be asked,' my old boss said.'" Adam paused a moment. "And now I'm going to pose them to you. The first is—did you get the job done?"

"Yes," she said firmly.

"The second—did you do anything illegal to get it done?"

"No."

"End of story. I wish I could say the same in my case."

"What happened?" she asked, relieved over his reaction to her admission.

Adam related his story, leaving out the tornado and bus driving episode for another time.

"Timmy sounds like a manipulator," Tamra noted.

"Well on his way to becoming a master manipulator."

"Is it possible that Manny could still be in Kansas City?"

"By now he could be anywhere."

"Colombia?"

"Anywhere but there. I doubt the goons would follow him to South America, even in the unlikely event he managed to escape there."

"Is this going to end up becoming our first cold case?" she asked.

"Private eyes normally don't accrue a lot of cold cases that originate with them," Adam pointed out. "We do, however, take up random law enforcement cold cases that have not been resolved over time at the request of families. We had a couple of those before you came on board. The majority of cold cases are homicides where the statutes of limitations don't apply. Besides, unresolved cheating spouse cases and the like are not worth the time and effort for us to pursue after a reasonable amount of time has passed. They have a short shelf life as do most of our cases, as you well know. What I fear is the Manny case may end up as a crime that never occurred in the eyes of the legal community."

"Manny should have known better than to skip out on his schooling and take up with gamblers," Tamra declared.

"Agreed, but from what little I know, he's basically a good kid who did not recognize the unsavory world he was operating in until it was too late. By the way, on that point, did I ever tell you about the Ballad of Teddy Lee?"

Tamra gave him a puzzled look. "The Ballad of Teddy Lee," she repeated. "No, I can't say you have. Is that a poem or a song?"

"Neither."

"Then why would you have told it to me, especially if it's not work-related?"

"Oh, but it is. Pete always used it as a prime example of how easily an innocent person can become entangled in a criminal activity."

"It was a case of his?"

"Yes...hold on," he said.

Adam walked back to a vintage filing cabinet stuck in the corner of the room and started to rifle through it.

"Adam, we need to get rid of that filing cabinet. I've entered most of the pertinent items in that cabinet into the computer. Everything thing else in there is ephemeral stuff."

"Ephemeral to you," he said, carrying a folder he had pulled from it back to the desk and plopping it down between the two of them.

"Do I really want to hear this?" she asked.

"I can sing it to you, if that would help."

"Oh, God no. Give it to me straight."

Adam nodded his agreement and proceeded to tell the tale of Teddy Lee. "Teddy was a professional librarian, straitlaced as they come. His first job was with the local public library system. Not long after he came on board, the library administration assigned him the task of compiling an illustrated, one-hundred-year history of the system in celebration of their upcoming centennial."

"Why him?" Tamra asked.

"Before he received his degree in library science, he worked as a copy editor for a newspaper. The administration thought his experience qualified him for the job. Anxious to please his new bosses he took it on, despite the limited funds he was allotted. To minimize expenditures, he recruited two co-workers to help him with the project. One was an amateur photographer on the side, the other the in-house artist. He recognized the bulk of the work would be digging through library archives to come up with appropriate historical photos. He knew there were more than enough of those. What he wanted was the unusual photograph that would add a little spice to the publication. After all, a history of the library has blandness written all over it...right?"

"For the uncultured, perhaps," Tamra retorted, "but not for the library patrons."

"Okay, I'll grant you that," Adam countered. "Anyway, after having sifted through the main library's archives, Teddy and the photographer decided to make a visit to the oldest branch in the system to see if they could dig up something out of the ordinary to add some juice to the project. When they asked the branch librarian if she knew of such an item, she hesitated for a moment, before telling them there was an old album buried in the files that they might be interested in. At their request she retrieved it and lo and behold, Teddy held in his hands the promise of the added zing he was in search of. Inside the album were a dozen or so individual photographs of librarians posing on a nearby hill...either against a tree, a large boulder, or rock ledge. It looked like something taken from an old Sears catalog. They were dressed in early 1900s fashion. What prompted the shoot was of no interest to Teddy. All he knew was that he had come up with what was to be the centerpiece of the illustrated history."

"What sorts of poses?" Tamra asked out of curiosity.

"Tasteful, yet something you wouldn't expect from members of a library staff."

"For what purpose, I wonder," Tamra pondered.

"No one seemed to know. Teddy could not have cared less what the purpose was. He was too busy rejoicing in his good fortune. To draw a distinction between the past and the present, he came up with the idea of inserting a similar photo of a current employee and what better place to do it than in the Central City Branch, the oldest branch in the system. Looking about, he spotted a woman's sun hat hanging on a coat rack near the library's entrance. 'Who does the hat belong to?' he asked the branch manager. 'Gabriella. We call her Gabby for short.' Teddy asked if she was on duty and was told she was on her break at the moment. 'Why do you ask?' the branch manager wanted to know. 'I would like to get a shot of her standing on your spiral staircase over there so we can insert her photo with the others to give it a then-and-now element.' The branch manager hunched her shoulders and smiled weakly. 'I'm not sure Gabby will easily go along with your idea, but you can run it by her...here she comes now.' As soon as he saw her, Teddy knew he had his gal. Tall, slender, and exceptionally attractive, she was wearing a burnt orange dress that buttoned down the front. Add a couple more feet of it and she would have been sporting a granny dress. Instead, it reached halfway down her thighs. It was the perfect outfit to juxtapose against the turn-of-the-century ladies."

"This has to do with a private investigation case?" Tamra asked skeptically.

"Hold on...I'm getting there."

Adam plucked the slim illustrated history from the folder he had retrieved and opened it to the fashion display. He turned the open book so Tamra could view the pages, carefully covering the photo of Gabby with the fingers of one hand.

Tamra viewed the photos with interest, curious as to whose idea it was to stage the shoot and how much backing there was for it from the staff. From the looks on their faces and poses, they appeared to be all in on it.

Adam removed his fingers from the Gabby photo, drawing Tamra's attention to the striking picture. If she had a reaction to it, she was doing a good job of disguising it, he thought. "Remind you of anyone?" he coyly asked.

"Nope," she replied in a matter-of-fact manner.

"Want me to get a mirror and hold it up to you?"

Tamra exhaled a deep breath. "Adam, get on with your story.

You say there is a lesson to be learned from it. I'm beginning to wonder if there's an end to it."

"Okay...okay. Part two coming up," he said, slipping the publication back into the file folder. "So, when Teddy got the developed photographs back, he made a point of asking those staff members in the contemporary photos for their permission to use them. He was particularly excited about showing Gabby the finished shots of her, confident she would give him the okay to run with them. At first, she feigned indifference toward their quality, but Teddy knew better. In fact, he was so full of confidence, he took things a step further, crossing the personal-professional divide by asking her for a dinner date after she approved them. She said yes to the dinner offer and with that came instant elation. He was officially on cloud nine. His book project was off the ground, as was his budding relationship with a girl whose beauty was the stuff of dreams."

"Why do I feel this storybook romance is headed in another direction," Tamra remarked, as she patiently waited for the turn of the tale.

"Because all good things must come to an end and so it did with Teddy, starting with his big night out with Gabby. Alas, the date turned out to be a dud. From the get-go, Gabby appeared greatly distracted. Teddy wasn't sure why. He didn't consider himself the cause of it or else why would she agree to go out with him in the first place? He thought perhaps she had a boyfriend and was unsettled by the thought she was stepping out on him. Whatever the reason, the disinterest on her part was enough for downhearted Teddy to decide there would be no second date. As he was leaving the modest duplex she lived in, he noticed a guy sitting in a car parked in front of it. More out of curiosity than caution he circled the block. By the time he completed it, the fellow was gone.

"The next morning, a few minutes before the library opened, a couple of staff members were hanging out around the reference desk chewing the fat when Teddy joined them. The local morning newspaper lay open on the desk. The topic under discussion was the series of front-page stories having to do with a nationally known doctor who was on trial for the alleged murder of his wife. Prosecutors accused him of injecting small doses of a rare, deadly form of poison into her system over a long period of time. Teddy was aware of the case but was not following it closely, despite it being the lead story on the local nightly newscasts. 'Did they ever determine a motive?' he asked the two staff members. 'Was it the insurance money?' Both staff members shook their head. 'You don't know?' one of them asked incredulously. Teddy in turn shook his head. 'There was another woman involved...a much younger one,' the staff member replied. 'You might know her. The rumor going around is that it's Gabriella Fontana who works at the Central City Branch.'

"Teddy was stunned, though it all made sense now. No wonder she was distracted. Her lover was on trial for his life. And what did the staff member mean when she said, 'You might know her.' Was she being coy? It dawned on him that he could easily be drawn into the story. Fittingly, he began receiving phone calls from news reporters regarding his relationship with her. Anonymous callers advised him to stay away from her. One guy, claiming to be a library personnel director in another system, said a female applicant had given him Teddy's name as a job reference and could he answer a few questions about her job performance. Teddy didn't want to go to the police with his concerns, or to Gabby, or to the library administration. What could they do? Get him and Gabby together for a strategy conference on how to keep the library's name out of it? The hell with that.

"Finally, a friend advised Teddy to consult with a lawyer to determine whether there were any legal liabilities he needed to be concerned about. 'However, before you go through the expense of hiring a lawyer, why don't you first check with this private eye friend of mine, His name is Pete Peterson. I understand the guy has lots of law enforcement contacts. He may be able to give you the inside scoop on the case and whether your involvement with Gabby is a cause for concern.'"

"Your old boss...Pete Peterson...the founder of this business?" Tamra interrupted.

"The same Pete Peterson," Adam said. "Through his contacts Pete was able to determine Gabby was in fact the doctor's paramour. However, she was not considered by the police an accomplice in his wife's alleged murder. Thus, she was never publicly named in the press as the other woman. Nonetheless, life at the library became a burden for Teddy. The rumor mill, conspiracy theories, and whispers reached frenzied levels. Teddy wasn't one to run and hide at the first sign of trouble, but the library administration was suspicious due to his rumored personal involvement with Gabby. It all came to a head when Teddy received his next performance evaluation. His supervisor advised him to be careful who he associated with on the staff...on or off the job. Teddy told him there was no need for him or the administration to worry because he wouldn't be around to associate with anyone. He had decided a change of scenery was in order. The Vietnam War was going on at the time and there was a good chance he would be drafted, so he ended up quitting his job to join the Air Force."

"I'm beginning to feel sorry for Teddy," Tamra said half in jest. "What was the outcome of the trial?"

"The doctor was found guilty."

"And Gabby?"

"Gabby also ended up quitting her job. From what I understand, she took a job up north."

"Do you happen to have a photo of Teddy in that file?" Tamra asked, nodding to the folder on the desk. "I've seen the one of Gabby. Now, I'm curious to see one of Teddy."

"You don't need to see a photo," Adam replied with a deadpanned look.

"Why is that?" she asked, her curiosity further stoked.

"Because you're looking at him."

Tamra cast him a side eye, quickly calculating the meaning of his response. "Adam Theodore Fraley...Teddy Lee. Where did the 'Lee' part come from?"

"My father's first name...remember?"

"Oh yeah," she drawled out. "I should have known."

"Following my stint in the Air Force, I enrolled in a criminal justice program at the university. While there, I noticed an ad in the paper for an office manager for a private investigator. It was Pete's office...the one we're sitting in. I applied and, much to my surprise, was given the job. The rest is history."

"So, you were the young, wide-eyed innocent ensnared in the criminal activity," she said with a grin. "Amazing, the little things you can learn about the man you're about to marry. And a onetime librarian to boot, albeit for a brief time. I would never have guessed."

"You find it surprising?"

"Yes, I do."

"In what way?"

"In a number of ways. Do I need to count them for you?"

Adam leaned across the desk. "One obviously being I have that sexy librarian look," he said through a roguish grin.

"Apparently, not sexy enough to sway Gabby to your side and away from the doctor," she countered.

"Okay, back to business," he said, rising from his chair to return the folder with the Ballad of Teddy Lee in it to the file cabinet.

The phone buzzed.

"I'm going to run to the post office to get the mail," he called out, as Tamra reached to grab the receiver.

The Manny Rivera case continued to weigh heavily on Adam's mind. Not only had he failed his client but Manny as well. On a hopeful note, it could turn out to be one of those cases where after a time...perhaps years...the kid will resurface somewhere with his life intact or a break in the case will occur out of the blue, leading to an eventual resolution of it. Little did he know that break would come the moment he returned to the office with the mail.

Tamra was sitting with her elbows propped on her desk and her hands clenched beneath her chin. It was a pose he had seen before from her, one that suggested something important was weighing on her mind.

"What's up?" he asked.

She released her hands from under her chin and motioned to

the chair across from her. "I think you should have a seat for this one."

"I could use a jolt of something...good or bad," he said, sliding into the chair.

"There's been a major development in both the Manny Rivera and the Wade Carson cases," she announced.

"In both cases? How so?"

"That incoming phone call I took when you headed off for the post office was from Carmen Rivera—Manny's mother."

"Oh yeah?" he said, perking up a bit from his funk.

"She told me the family has received an anonymous call from a man informing them they had Manny in their possession and that they were to send $50,000 in U.S. dollars in five separate manila envelopes to gain his release. They instructed her to conceal the money with paper so as not to draw attention to the envelopes and to make sure there is sufficient postage."

Adam paused a moment to absorb the news. "By all means...'don't forget to put the stamps on the envelopes' say the geniuses of international money transfer," he chaffed. "Send it where?"

"To an M. Rivera at a post office box number here in Tampa."

"Did they send it?"

"Not yet. They wanted to talk to us first."

"She didn't tell the caller that, I hope."

"No. She told them she would need a little time to liquidate some assets into cash. I told her we would get back to her shortly."

"Does she have any idea where the call came from and who the caller was?"

"Here's the kicker, Adam. Initially, she had no idea. However, her husband happens to be an executive for the phone company in Colombia. He checked the records. It came from Florida...Tampa to be precise...the Ybor City section."

"You don't mean..."

"Yes, the number belonged to Wade Carson. Adam, when I was over at his place working the case, he asked why you hadn't accompanied me to the island. I told him you were on a case in

Kansas City. He mentioned he had made several visits there on business. Considering his involvement with the underworld, it doesn't require too much speculation to connect him to the mob activities in KC, Las Vegas, and by extension to the gambling activities of Manny Rivera and his cohorts, does it?"

"Not at all," he replied, energized by the new development. "It appears our two investigations have come crashing into each other. The question now is, where is Manny being held...KC? Florida?"

"I can give you one possibility," Tamra advanced.

"Let's hear it."

"Mickey Riley...Susan Carson's brother, mentioned to me during the initial interview with him there were a couple of guys living in Wade Carson's permanent residence in Ybor City..."

"Where the number was traced to."

"Yes...when I checked the real estate records at the time, he was still listed as the owner. Could be it was the mob's henchmen doing the house sitting."

"And now the babysitting," Adam chimed in. "At this juncture we need to set up a meeting with Jim Alexander at the FBI office as soon as possible. I'll give him a call. Meanwhile, why don't you return Carmen Rivera's call and ask her to hold off sending the ransom money until she hears back from us."

"They're going to be under enormous pressure to send it, Adam."

"I know, but considering all of the legal boundaries being crossed, this clearly is a case calling for the FBI's involvement before we make another move. Tell Carmen we will get back to her by the end of the day. Should they call her again, suggest she tell them she needs a little more time to liquidate the assets."

An hour later they were sitting in Jim Alexander's office. Exceedingly careful and serious in his manner, Adam and Tamra found him to be an enormous help in working with him on a previous case. When they finished relating their story, the FBI man concurred with the advice they gave Mrs. Rivera to hold off with the ransom payment. He also agreed with Tamra's speculation as to where Manny was being held. "Kansas City and the Bahamas are too distant from where the ransom call was made," he said. "Given the logistics, Carson's permanent home is the likely spot. I'm going to round up a few agents to make a visit to the Ybor City location first. Oh, one other thing," he said, turning to Tamra. "You said Mickey Riley escorted his sister from the rental house. Do you know where he took her? Hopefully, not back to the Ybor City residence. We don't want her to be anywhere near the site, much less showing up when we make our visit."

"I made a follow-up call to him earlier today to ask him the same question," said Tamra. "He said she's staying with him for the time being. I suggested he not take her back there until we determine who the two guys holed up in the home are. I advised him they are under suspicion by federal authorities and that his sister could be in danger until matters are settled."

"Good...I believe we are all set then."

"You want us to tag along with you?" Adam asked.

"Yes, for identification purposes. You, Tamra, along with me and another agent will take one van, while two other agents follow us in a backup."

"Are you going to need a search warrant?" Tamra asked.

"We've already obtained one right after Adam called," Alexander replied. "It doesn't take long. Time is critical in kidnapping cases. Judges realize this and usually act according to our wishes. We may not even need to show it. I doubt the perpetrators will even insist on one, especially if they're a couple of henchmen, as you say, and not the owners of the place. I expect them to be cooperative. Most people are when we come calling."

The fact that Alexander had the build of an NFL defensive lineman might have something to do with the cooperative attitudes, Adam figured.

CHAPTER ELEVEN

WADE CARSON'S PERMANENT RESIDENCE WAS A TWO-STORY structure, colored a pastel blue and white, with a sizable front porch and short flight of steps running up to it. A gravel driveway led to a garage in the back. A brown Lincoln Town Car was parked in it. The avenue the house was located on was a quiet, tree-lined one, far removed from the more heavily trafficked areas. A few vehicles were parked on the street. All appeared unoccupied. The house itself was situated in the middle of the block.

Altogether, it was a beautiful day in the neighborhood for an FBI raid. Unfortunately, it was also a beautiful day for a pickup football game, as evidenced by the group of young boys who, without warning, came scrambling out from behind one of the houses to the street to begin a three on three contest. They couldn't have chosen a worst spot on the block to disrupt the FBI's plans—directly in front of the target house.

"Well, this is something we didn't plan on," Alexander snapped, grabbing the car phone in frustration. "I take it you see what's going on in front of us?" he barked to the agents in the backup van behind them. "Let's put things on hold for the moment," he said in resignation.

All eyes in the van were rotating between the youngsters engaged in the game and the windows of the target house to see if the schoolyard chatter was drawing the attention of its occupants. None was observed, even though one errant pass sailed into the front yard of the house where it was quickly retrieved by one of the kids.

"If this doesn't end soon, we may have to postpone the mission to another day, which I sure as hell do not want to do, given the time constraints we're operating under," Alexander said.

They continued to divide their attention between the target house windows and the game, except the game they had uppermost in their minds was not football.

"Jim, can I borrow that clipboard you have stashed on your dash?" Tamra abruptly asked.

Eyes turned from the street scene to the woman in the rear seat.

"Sure," Alexander hesitantly said, snatching the clipboard and handing it back to her. Before anyone could ask, "Why?" she opened the back door and stepped out of the van, leaving everyone, including Adam, flummoxed.

"What does she have in mind?" Alexander asked.

"Damned if I know," Adam responded.

Tamra walked the half block to where the boys were playing, boldly approaching them from the sidewalk. "Say, fellows," she called out, capturing their attention. "Can I ask a favor of you?"

Their game interrupted, the boys eyeballed each other, before giving her a collective nod.

She glanced at the clipboard to give an air of officiality to what she was about to say "A government crew will be working this street shortly. We would appreciate it, if you could move your game somewhere else, perhaps the next block down."

She was hoping they didn't ask, "What kind of work?" Fudging the truth was one thing. Telling an outright falsehood was another. Lying did not come easy to her. Fortunately, they didn't ask for the details, much to her relief.

"Sure, we can move," one of the boys said to her request and off they went, tossing the football back and forth among them on their jaunt down to the next block.

Tamra casually strolled back to the van and hopped back into the back seat, receiving a pat on the shoulder from Adam.

Alexander was at once back on the phone to the backup van, "Let's do it."

The agents wasted no time in carrying out the operation. While Alexander and the other agent in the van stepped quickly to the front door, the two agents from the backup van circled to the rear of the house. Alexander rapped on the front door and stood to the side of it. A minute later he reached out and rapped a second time. The knocks could clearly be heard from the backseat of the van Adam and Tamra occupied.

The door finally opened and in a self-inviting move, the two agents had their feet inside the house before the greeter must have realized what was happening. The door closed and Adam, Tamra, along with an elderly neighbor lady who had been peeking between her window curtains at the goings on, were back to playing the waiting game.

It felt like an hour had passed to Adam, though a check of his watch indicated it was half that in real time when the door reopened. Out stepped the two henchmen, and not just any two henchmen. It was Cory Hoagland and the accordion guy, minus his instrument. "Well...well..., if it isn't my two traveling companions," he said to Tamra. The two were led away in handcuffs by the backup agents who escorted them to their vehicle. Adam viewed it as neither a good or bad indicator of what was to come. Moments later, Alexander and the remaining agent exited the home with Manny between them.

"Is that Manny?" Tamra asked.

"That's Manny," he replied, barely able to contain his glee.

"Good call, Tamra," Alexander said as he and the other agent climbed into the front seat, leaving the jump seat for Manny. On seeing Adam, Manny appeared to recognize him immediately. "You were the guy on the bus, the one who took it over when that twister was headed our way," he said.

All eyes in the vehicle were redirected to Adam for an explanation. "That's a story for another day," he said, dismissing it with a grin.

They drove to the FBI office where the two accomplices were placed in custody. Manny's mother was called and notified her son was in the hands of the agency and that they would be contacting her later to fill her in on the details.

"Are there any charges he might be facing?" Tamra asked, back in Alexander's office.

"Big difference between owing money to an illegal gambling activity and a legitimate one," he pointed out. From what we know so far, I seriously doubt the former will be coming out of the shadows to officially charge him with anything. They would be placing themselves at risk by exposing their operation.

"When do we launch stage two?" Adam asked.

"As soon as I round up a crew. Meanwhile, let's hope the afternoon results are as good as this morning's outcome."

"Any chance Carson's been tipped off?" Adam asked.

"I doubt it," the FBI man said. "Certainly not by those two goons we brought in. They were caught completely by surprise from the looks on their faces when we entered."

―――――

"Is that his vehicle parked in the drive?" Alexander asked upon their arrival at Carson's rental home in Boca Grande.

"Yes," Tamra answered from the rear seat she and Adam were sharing once again.

"Okay, let's pay him a visit," Alexander said to the agent sitting aside him. They were at once followed by the backup agents in the trailing van. Their approach was the same as it was in Tampa. Alexander and the number two agent strode directly to the front door while the backups headed to the rear. Alexander pounded on the door and stepped aside. There was no response. He pounded a second and third time, calling out "FBI...open the door!" on the third attempt. Still no response. He walked to the rear of the home to consult with the other two agents. When finished he headed back to the van, sliding open the rear door to address Tamra. "How well do you know this guy?"

"I knew him well years ago. He's a former boyfriend of mine. As I mentioned in our background briefing, I came in contact with him again during the course of an investigation into his wife's disappearance. I have since learned he was rumored to have ties to the underworld."

"Okay, here's the situation," Alexander said in his drill-like manner. "He's a suspect. His car is parked in the drive. He is not responding to our presence for whatever reason. There's the possibility he's in some sort of imminent danger. I tell you this because we are going to force our way in. Do either of you have any objection to our doing so?"

Both glanced at each other, shrugged, and shook their heads no, ostensibly surprised they were even asked. On second thought, it was probably wise of them to get any objections on the record prior to taking action, Adam figured. After all, they stood to be witnesses to the event should anything go awry.

The four agents gathered behind the house where they would make their forced entry, Adam surmised. He and Tamra were back to playing the waiting game, a role that was fast becoming a chore.

"Come to think of it, he could be walking the beach," Tamra said, annoyed by her overlooking the obvious. "Dare I go mention this to them?"

"By now, they're in. If he does come walking up the street, let them deal with the consequences."

Adam sensed the unease in her. For Tamra this was personal. How much so, only she could answer and he was not about to ask.

A half hour had passed when Alexander stepped out the front door and motioned for the two to come join them.

"We're officially operating under the do-not-contaminate rule," Alexander said as he led them into the home. His words raised an entirely new level of concern for the two private investigators.

"Is he here?" Tamra asked expectantly.

"He is and he isn't," Alexander answered, continuing with his cryptic comments.

"Meaning what?" Adam asked with a tinge of annoyance.

"Meaning he's dead."

Adam glanced at his partner who was doing her best to disguise her shock.

They followed the agent up a stairwell to the second floor and entered an alcove that had been converted into a home office. A plain wooden desk and chair were positioned in front of a large bay window that provided a clear view of the Gulf. Off to one side of the alcove stood an open bookshelf lined with legal tomes. However, it was the desk and chair that held everyone's attention at the moment. Slumped in the chair with his head resting on the desk and a gun clutched in his right hand was the deceased. A substantial accumulation of dried blood blotted the top of the desk.

He was still wearing the same clothes he had worn early this morning, Tamra noted.

"Is this Wade Carson?" Alexander asked of her.

"Yes," she said in a whisper.

Looking at the lifeless body, Tamra could not help but note the stark contrast between the dead calm atmosphere of the home and the highly charged one of yesterday. As much as she would have liked to put the Wade Carson matter behind her, she did not wish or expect it to end like this. *Rescue me!* The words reverberated in her mind, spawning disturbing questions. Was she at all responsible for his death? Was the note he sent to her at the restaurant in fact a plea from him for help? Should she have recognized the mental state he was in, especially this morning, and displayed more empathy toward him?

"Self-inflicted, I presume," Adam said.

"Looks that way," Alexander replied, standing aside the desk with his hands to his hips in a contemplative pose. "Appears to be a single shot to the head. Gun's still in his hand which is common when the person is in a sitting position. Nor is there evidence of a struggle or break-in, except for the one executed by us," he added with a quick grin. "Given his recent history, it's probably not all that surprising he chose this way out."

Adam saw a mix of consternation and sadness settle on Tamra's face and thought no matter the circumstances of the parting of a past girlfriend or boyfriend, they take a piece of you with them when they leave for the final time. He sensed her heightened anxiety. Whether out of habit, enhanced familiarity, or strong emotional attachment, he was able at this stage of their relationship to dial into her thoughts. Hence, he asked of Alexander the question he knew to be on her mind. "Did he leave a suicide note?"

"None we could find. Normally, when they do, they leave it out in the open so it won't be overlooked," he answered.

"I once saw one spray painted on a wall," one of the other agents inspecting the room called out, attempting to bring a little levity to the scene.

Alexander exhaled a deep breath and removed his hands from his hips. "It's been a long day. How about I give you two a ride back to the office and your vehicle? The other agents will remain here until the medical examiner and local cops arrive. I'll touch base with you later, once we get an official reading on this."

As they exited the island, Tamra realized the charming, natural tropical images she always associated with the little town of Boca Grande would forever be tainted by images of another kind...man-made ones.

———

ON THE RIDE back from the FBI office, Adam popped the question that had been nagging him. "Did you find this entire episode today somewhat strange?"

Tamra turned to the man behind the wheel, "Strange in what way?"

"First of all, why did Carson make the ransom call? Wouldn't he want to maintain a public distance from the mob when it came to blatant illegal activity? It begs the question of whether the actual perpetrators of the crime knew he was making the contact. A call from one of the major players would have been more in line with the way these things go down. Secondly, he must have known there was a reasonable chance the call could be traced to his Tampa residence and that some bright person like my office manager would immediately point to his home there as a possible staging area for the kidnapping. I don't know, but it almost seems like he gifted the thing to us."

"He did," she said with certainty. "It was a wedding gift, Adam... a one-of-a-kind wedding present."

He took his eyes off the road for a moment to give her a puzzled look. "You serious?"

"Trust me on this one, Adam," she said. "Besides, we got the job done—right?"

"Right."

"And we did nothing illegal---right?"

"Nothing that I can recall offhand."

"As someone in this car famously said not so long ago—"end of story.'"

———

LATER IN THE evening Adam was on the phone with his former boss and longtime mentor, Pete Peterson, recounting two recent events he considered problematic---the Manny case and the offer from The Justice Brigade. The Carson case he would leave out, for there was little to chew over from a professional perspective. As for the personal side of it, he was of a mind to put it aside for the time being. "The floor is yours," he said to his mentor, following his rundown.

"Which do you want me start with?" Peterson asked.

"Let's go with the Manny case first."

"Congrats to you. I really don't see much more you could have done. The kid was lost, found, lost, then found again. For a while there, it sounded like it had all the makings of a cold case, one of those where years down the line, the kid would pop up somewhere, maybe as President of Peru, or head of a drug cartel, or your friendly next-door neighbor. Whichever or wherever, it was wise of you not to pick a fight with the mob, my friend. You don't have the resources nor the savvy for it. Always let the FBI fight it out with them, if they choose to do so. As for the business proposition made to you by The Justice Brigade, I'm glad you asked..."

"You are the founder of this operation, Pete. How could I not ask?" he interjected. You have a vested interest in the place."

"A sentimental one, more than anything else," he noted. "By the way, that word *founder* makes me sound very old. But back to the point...I've never known you to be a materialistic guy, Adam. You're a blue collar, one-car, one-house, one-woman man. You like to live comfortably, not extravagantly. You say it's a lucrative offer, yet my question is...is it you? You love your independence, especially when it comes to running your business. It's the first thing you will be sacrificing if you enter into some kind of merger. You either own yourself or let someone else own you. Also, keep in mind you're a businessman first and a private investigator second. It follows you can be an average P.I. and excellent businessman and make a go of it. On the other hand, you can't be a below average businessman, no matter how good a P.I. you are, and still keep the operation afloat. Sure, it can be a simple joining of forces, something along the lines of a retainer-type agreement, but remember...who controls the money controls you. Once a firm like The Justice Brigade gets a piece of you, they will eventually swallow you up and assimilate you into their corporate structure where chances are you will end up as just another cog in their wheel. What if they decide to reorganize a month after you're on board and notify Tamra she's being transferred to another position in another department?"

"I don't expect that to happen, Pete. Many of the points you bring up could be addressed in the contractual details, eliminating any sudden surprises."

"Ask those who've worked in the world of big business how often they experienced the unexpected. And do you really want to go head to head over contractual obligations with a law firm? Have you run this by Tamra?"

"I did."

"Her reaction?"

"Initially, much the same as yours."

"Initially? You mean you talked her into the idea?"

"No, not at all. She was skeptical."

"Evidence, as if it were needed, to how smart of a woman she is."

"The Justice Brigade's contact person recently sweetened the pot. He informed me the firm is now offering scholarships to children of their employees. No matter what the final contractual relationship is agreed upon, Noelle would be eligible."

"Those corporate scholarships pale in comparison to the scholarships offered by colleges or foundations. Noelle is a bright young lady. She should have no trouble landing an academic scholarship, or an athletic one, for that matter. She also could work part time for you, could she not? Which brings up another possibility. Why not grow your own business? You could expand it to include a security service for homeowners and private businesses alike. You could also offer an internship to one of those grad students working toward a degree in criminal justice. They could help around the office, which would free you and Tamra up to take on the extra workload."

"That's another thing, Pete. Like every other endeavor, technology has dramatically changed the profession since you were running the show. It's almost to the point where you have to make a choice between desktop investigations or on-site surveillance."

"There's no reason you still can't do both...do the computer searches and still work the phone and canvass the streets. It appears to me you're already experimenting along those lines. It's a matter of you two proportioning your time."

"So, it's a no vote coming from you on the merger proposal?"

"I don't get a vote, nor should I."

"Your advice then."

"Tell them thanks for the offer and that you highly value them as a customer, but prefer to keep the working relationship as is. That is my advice. As always, do with it what you will."

"I'm always impressed with how you can look at life in simple terms, Pete. How'd you develop that clarity?"

"I've taken to watching the old classic westerns in my golden years—you know, back when men were men, women were women, and horses were horses. Lines of behavior were clearly drawn during those times. Cross them and the consequences were immediate. You walk into a saloon and the guy sitting across the table from you decides he doesn't like your looks, or something you said, or something you did, and the next thing you know he's challenging you to a duel. Looking down the barrel of a gun will instill lucidity in you faster than anything."

"One thing I've never asked you, Pete. How did you get started in this business?"

"A good buddy of mine wanted to open up a P.I. office. He needed some start-up money, so I loaned him some. A day before the business was to open, he was killed in a car crash. I was painting houses at the time and bored out of my mind, so rather than let my money go to complete waste, I decided to try my hand at the business, despite having zero experience in it. My sole knowledge of the trade came from watching the TV crime shows. In any event, on the first day I opened for business, this eccentric, little old lady walks into my office off the street and wants to hire me to tail her multi-millionaire husband to Lake Tahoe where he's planning on attending a week-long reunion with his Korean War buddies. She doesn't trust him...believes he might have a honey or two on the side. However, that's not the kicker to the story. The woman's husband had total control of the family finances. She had no money of her own to pay me, but that didn't stop her. She went to him and threatened a very messy divorce—a lifestyle altering one —if he didn't provide her the money. And he did."

"Knowing it would be used to hire you to tail him to Tahoe?"

"Yep, at her insistence the guy was willing to let her pick the P.I. of her choice. All she wanted in return for the service was a written daily account of her husband's activities. In other words, I got an all-expense-paid trip to Tahoe, including my hourly fee, to basically hang out with this guy and his military vet buddies for a week."

"Lots of fun stuff, huh?"

"If you call hanging around the hotel bar, pool, and restaurant listening to old war stories fun stuff."

"There was no hanky-panky in your final report."

"None whatsoever. I felt in the end like I had saved a marriage."

"And that was your first case?"

"First one, and I was inexperienced enough to think that if this is what the business is like, give me more of it. Sad to say, it turned out to be the least challenging and most lucrative case of my career. It was all downhill in terms of difficulty from then on."

"You were always the decisive guy, as I recall. I remember the first time I walked into your office looking for a job with Pete Peterson's Private Investigations. There was no resume required... no background check...no personal references...and little job experience to consider, yet you hired me on the spot. I know small business owners had more discretionary power back in those days, but all the same, it was you who started me down this career path for which I will always be grateful."

"Before you get all gushy about the hire my friend, I should remind you that it was a desperate hire at the time for many pressing reasons that are no longer worth discussing. Suffice it to say, I threw the equivalent of a Hail Mary pass and somehow it worked," his old boss playfully said, the smile on his face easily discerned from the other end of the line.

CHAPTER TWELVE

"Found it!" his office manager shouted out first thing the next morning.

"Found what?" Adam asked.

"Here...I'll read it to you. 'A passenger aboard a bus bound for Kansas City from Wichita took over the wheel for a suddenly incapacitated driver during a severe storm system that swept through the region yesterday. The passenger, who wished to remain anonymous, at one point maneuvered the bus from the path of a twister that was about to intersect the highway they were traveling. "He seemed to know what he was doing," one of the other passengers said...'"

Tamra lowered her gaze from the computer screen and cupped her mouth with a free hand to smother a chuckle.

"My extracurricular activity appears to be cheering you up. Obviously, you don't agree I knew what I was doing," Adam said from across the room, pleased to see the mirth back in her.

"Well, did you?" she needled.

"Someday, I'll tell you about my bus driving experiences in the military. They are legendary."

Tamra returned her attention to the article. "There's an accompanying photo here of the passenger who gave the quote."

Curious as to whom it might be, he stepped across the room, pulled up a chair across from her desk and leaned in for a view. 'Oh, yeah, a bright young nursing student. She took care of the regular driver while I took control of the bus."

Tamra printed the page. "Your daughter needs to learn of her father's daring heroics. I'll save this for her."

"As of this morning, my daughter is home from her camping trip."

"You say that as if you're not sure it's a good thing."

"Oh, I'm glad to have her back. It's just that kids of her age are so impressionable. All it takes is a new hands-on experience to set them off in a new direction in life."

"Which direction?"

"Any which way, as long as it's aimed at saving the planet. Apparently, the trip revived her interest in pursuing global humanitarian causes. I told her she first needed to focus on her education before she takes on the world."

"Noelle balked at that? It doesn't sound like her. She has always put her education first."

"She says she can do both. I advised her to take it up with you."

"With me?"

"Sure...soon she will be your daughter also, so you might as well get in a little prenuptial training for it. Plus, aren't you now focusing simultaneously on the two branches of our business---office and field work?"

Tamra refused to get drawn into the comparison. "Did you speak with your old boss about the proposed Justice Brigade merger?"

"Yes, I did, and he's on your side with this one. The more I bounce it around in my head, the less enthusiastic I am about the potential benefits, so much so, I feel we should no longer pursue the matter. I'll let them know our decision."

"Regarding the business at hand, you received a call from the

Kansas City Police Department...from a Sergeant Kendall," she said, handing a note to him. It has to do with the Manny case...a follow-up call it sounds like. Were they working on something for you?"

"Not that I know of. I'll give him a ring back," he said, returning to his desk to make the call.

Kendall was at his desk when Adam's call was switched through to him. "Yes, Mr. Fraley. I was interested in learning whether Manny Rivera ever showed up on your end."

"Yes, he did, as a matter of fact." Adam gave him a brief outline of what led to locating him and the assistance they received from the local FBI office.

"Good—glad to hear that. It may be a moot point now, but I was also calling to let you know I conducted a cursory follow-up investigation and was able to obtain some information from the bus company regarding the ride you took from Wichita to Kansas City. I even spoke to the agent at the Las Vegas station who handled the original counter ticket sales. She recalled clearly the two individuals you described as Manny's kidnappers. According to their records, the accordion guy's name was Steve Conrad, the pony-tailed fellow was Cory Hoagland. All she had on the record were their end destination—Kansas City—and names. She saw nothing out of the ordinary. We checked the names here, real or not, and found no outstanding warrants on either of the two. That's not to say they've not run afoul of the law in the past, just that there was not sufficient evidence for us to launch a full-scale probe."

"I understand. But you say they had no record of their home addresses?"

"Correct...no street addresses, only their end destinations, that being Kansas City. One other item she mentioned I found interesting. The three appeared to be traveling together. They all requested seats next to empty ones so they could stretch out. In addition, she faxed me a seating chart for the Wichita to KC route with the names of the passengers filled in. I can fax a copy to you for your records, if you like. As I said, it may all be a moot point now."

"Yes, I would like to have a copy for our records."

Adam gave him their fax number and thanked him for his input. Like the sergeant, he considered the info about the three appearing to be traveling together, an eyebrow raiser, if not a game changer.

In the background the fax machine sprung to life, churning out the seating chart. Adam retrieved it and returned to his desk to peruse the document. With the fresh info in hand, he launched into a total review of the trip. Upon reflection, four images stood out to him in a new light. Manny sitting next to Conrad and Hoagland on the bench in Emporia and engaging them in a short conversation while occasionally casting quick glances, as though they were looking for someone. Secondly, Hoagland introducing himself to him on the bus using a name, fake or not. Thirdly, Manny being pushed by the other two into the van at the KC bus station. Was he really being pushed or was he simply being hurried along by the other two? Fourthly, did the two actually hand over Manny to someone else at the airport or were they taking the cab to another terminal after having seen Manny off on another flight? Had they arranged the van ride from the bus station to the airport in advance? And did Manny actually fly to Tampa on his own, considering his paralyzing fear of flying?

Adam repeatedly reviewed the events in his mind before coming to a conclusion.

He turned to his office manager. "Tamra...can I ask you to drop what you're working on to do me a favor?"

"Sure, what is it?"

"I'd like for you to call Mickey Riley and ask him if he can ask his sister this question. Did her husband know beforehand the guys they rented their house to?"

"I thought we already knew the answer to that," she responded.

"We surmised it. We didn't verify it."

She started to ask a follow-up question but thought it best to first carry out his instruction.

Adam sat and listened patiently as she made the call. When finished she passed him the answer. "Mickey asked his sister and she told him neither she nor her husband knew the renters beforehand."

A brief silence ensued before Adam responded. "We got it all wrong, Tamra, or I should say that I got it all wrong."

"What do you mean...the Manny case?"

"Yes, the Manny case. Wade Carson was not involved in the ransom plot at all. Steve Conrad, the accordion guy, Cory Hoagland, the pony-tailed guy, Timmy Stacy, the little manipulator, and Manny himself, together hatched the plan to bilk Manny's parents out of $50,000. There was no underworld gambling mob chasing after them."

"How did you arrive at that conclusion?"

"Holes in the story kept cropping up, beginning with the notion Wade Carson made the ransom call from his Tampa home. Why wouldn't he make the call from his rental home in Boca Grande, if he indeed was the one who actually made it? Why drive all the way to Tampa to do it? In fact, there is no evidence he was ever at his Tampa home during this period or as we just learned, that he even knew any of the plotters."

"Okay, who made the call if not him?"

"Any of them could have other than Manny. Sure, he could have disguised his voice but why take that chance? Let another do it."

"All of them went to Vegas?"

"Yes...all of them. They were hell-bent on spending as much of the Rivera family's money as they could, courtesy of their son and the funds given him for his education. No doubt the parents had provided him a credit card or two as well. Yeah, the gang ended up doing just that---blowing it all. That led them to come up with the idea of milking Manny's parents for more."

"You said you saw them hauling Manny away at the KC bus station," Tamra pointed out.

"Now that I think of it, they weren't shoving him into the van as much as rushing him into it. He was the baby of the bunch, totally submissive to their whims, including the ransom idea."

"What about the run-in with them at the KC airport?"

"They didn't turn Manny over to a third party. More than likely they saw him off on a flight and were in the process of taking the airport taxi to another concourse to catch another flight...for what reason I do not know. Since they were low on funds, it could have been for financial reasons, booking issues, or time factors. The only thing I can't figure out is how Manny boarded a plane, considering his paranoia about flying."

"Maybe his fear of getting caught in a crime trumped his fear of flying."

"Possible. Whatever, they all ended up in Tampa."

"Do you think they knew who you were all along? Manny seemed surprised to see you when he was picked up in Tampa."

"It was feigned. I'm now convinced they all knew from the beginning. When I was over at Timmy's and identified who I was, I'm positive he contacted them at the Vegas bus station to let them know a private investigator by the name of Adam Fraley was on their tail. Undoubtedly, he provided them a description. While on the bus, Hoagland, who was sitting right across the aisle from me, introduced himself with a handshake, giving his full name, a subtle way of influencing me to give my full name in return, which I instinctively did. There was a reason they asked for separate seats and it was not to stretch their legs. They wanted to up their chances of identifying the private eye on board."

"You're thinking Timmy was the ringleader?"

"I'm sure of it."

"Adam, you had no idea anyone on that bus would recognize your name," she said in support.

He nodded his agreement. "There was another incident that comes to mind. While we were stuck in Emporia and lounging around waiting for the replacement bus to arrive, I noticed Manny sitting at a bench with Hoagland and Conrad. There appeared to be some casual chatter between the three. It didn't surprise me all that much at the time...just a few passengers killing time. But then I saw all three suddenly looking about as though they were trying to locate someone. I now believe that someone was me. They were acting like they had become aware they might be arousing my suspicion."

"You were where at the time?"

"In a nearby roadside cafe, drinking coffee. I had a nice view of the outside surroundings."

"To think Wade Carson was not involved at all, except for the happenstance of renting out his home to this group, comes as a big surprise to me, Adam. You weren't the only one wrong. I was the one who originally suggested his involvement."

"A natural conclusion to come to, considering his ties to the gambling mob. Yet, now we know there is no proof he had a connection to the plotters."

"His visits to KC?"

"Random business trips...for purposes unrelated to this case, in my opinion."

"What about the plotters? Could they have been aware of their landlord's gambling connections?"

"I believe it was pure chance they rented a home owned by a lawyer who happened to have ties to the underworld. Not all that unusual when you think about it. Those ties can cover a lot of territory."

"A fortunate happenstance, for sure."

"Breaks in cases are more often than not serendipitous. For us it turned out to be the one we needed. For them, it was another bad roll of the dice. Still, I feel like I was outsmarted for the most part by that little shyster Timmy and his three buddies. The sad part is, it didn't take too many smarts on their part to almost pull it off."

"And here I thought Carson was deliberately gifting a solution to us," she said, admitting her mistaken notion.

Her referring to Carson by his last name did not escape Adam. He took it as a subtle sign of the fissure that occurred in her relationship with the guy. Women generally don't refer to someone with whom they've had a personal connection by their last name, unless a fissure in it had occurred. Maybe, he was making too much of it...or perhaps not enough.

"The only gift-giving he was doing was to himself," he said in answer to her comment. "He bought a cheap ticket out of whatever torment he was living in."

Whatever torment he was living in, she repeated to herself, unsettled by the lingering idea she may have greatly contributed to the torment. "So, what now?" she asked.

"This calls for a hasty visit to Jim Alexander's office to tell him what I just told you."

CHAPTER THIRTEEN

JIM ALEXANDER LISTENED TO ADAM'S REVISED STORY WITH A half-smile on his face, as though he'd half expected it.

"We're a step ahead of you, Adam. Our agents questioned Steve Conrad and Cory Hoagland. They fessed up to the whole scheme. By the way, those are their real names."

"Are they all in custody?"

"Yes...charges are pending."

"What about that little manipulator Timmy Stacy?"

"Him, too. Two of our agents are at this moment bringing him in from Sarasota. The three of them were all pals who found a patsy in Manny. They introduced him to the wild side of life to which he became addicted. To feed his addiction and that of his so-called buddies, he agreed to their scheme to fleece his parents."

"I still have one question that puzzles me," Adam said. "They were essentially broke after they blew all of Manny's parents' money in Vegas. Yes, they still had a little money left over for the bus trip, but how did they manage to cover the cost of the air fares from Kansas City to Tampa, as well as Timmy's from Vegas to Tampa?"

"We asked that very question. The answer is they all went the parental route, except for Manny who did not want to contact his parents for fear of having his location disclosed. That would have raised more troubling questions for them as to what he was up to. Timmy got his parents to cover his flight from Vegas to Tampa, while Hoagland milked his parents for his and Conrad's flight back from Kansas City. At his request Hoagland's parents even arranged to have the rental van at the KC bus station to take them to the airport. As for Manny getting the funds to fly, the others all chipped in for his ticket."

"Regarding Manny...what's in store for him?" Adam asked.

"Manny requires a different kind of treatment. He's a foreign resident, temporarily living here. The question is---did he commit a crime against his own family while on U.S. soil? The next question is---do the parents want to press charges against him here or in their own country...or do we want to file charges no matter his parents' wishes? The legal people will have to sort it all out. If convicted of a crime, he will be subject to deportation. My inclination is to send him back to Colombia and let the family and the government there handle him one way or the other. In any case, it is now out of your hands. By the way, the medical examiner has officially ruled Wade Carson's death a suicide."

Adam acknowledged the news with a nod of the head. "I'll pass the ruling on to Tamra."

"'An old boyfriend whom she recently reconnected with over on the island,' she said to me. How's she handling the situation?"

"As you said on the last case we worked together, Jim. 'She's a trooper.'"

"WELL, DID HE BUY YOUR REVISION?" Tamra asked upon his return from the FBI office.

Adam lowered himself into a chair across the desk from her. "He had no choice but to buy it. The gang of four had already owned up to the plot by the time I arrived at his office."

"What charges are they going to bring against them?"

"That's still up in the air until the prosecutors sort out what they can and cannot do given the circumstances. The international element muddies matters. Alexander is of a mind to ship Manny back home to Colombia and let his parents and government decide what to do with him."

"Your preference is?"

"My preference is irrelevant now that our part is essentially over. We found the missing persons...our charge from the beginning. By the way, Alexander informed me the medical examiner has ruled Wade Carson's death a suicide, caused by a self-inflicted gunshot wound to the head."

He watched her reaction closely. It amounted to a slight shrug and a shifting of her eyes away from him. He waited patiently for their return. When they did, he locked onto them. "Tell me...what is it?"

"I can't help but think I somehow contributed to his death."

"For being who you are?"

Adam recalled the sage advice his old boss gave him, following their engagement and the prospect of their business becoming a mom-and-pop operation. "Don't let any issue rise above your love for each other," he had said. Adam was not about to let that happen. He reached across the desk and took her hand. "The responsibility lies with him, Tamra. His thoughts...his actions...not yours...drove him to the grave. It was his decision. I've never known you to wish harm on anyone."

She nodded, her eyes mirroring her uncertainty.

He was ready to continue with his argument but didn't. He knew when the time was right and the matter settled in her mind, she would share her thoughts with him, just as she had always done in the past.

She leaned forward to whisper to him. "Adam. I have a request to make. It may be a little out of line..."

"Let's hear it."

"Would you be opposed to moving our wedding date up a couple of weeks?"

He smiled. "Do you expect me to oppose that?" he asked without questioning why she would make such an offer.

"I wasn't sure. We were planning a small wedding anyway, so I figured it wouldn't take a great deal of re-planning to move it up."

"I'm all in favor," he said. "However, I do have a request in return."

Her eyes widened. "I'm listening."

"We've never discussed our honeymoon plans. So, here's what I propose. I know how much you like long walks. My legs and lungs can attest to it. Well, I recently learned of a place where you can walk forever, through gently rolling hills, pathways bordered by wildflowers of nearly every sort, and grasses taller than a full-grown man, where overhead you can watch the hawks and eagles ride the thermals and puffs of white clouds slowly float by..."

"Along with the occasional twister," she teasingly interjected in a sign of her old self.

"Yes, you can also watch the occasional tornado pass by, but don't worry, the hero guy you were reading about in the article this morning will be there to save you. By the way, I haven't even gotten to the meandering creeks and hidden waterfalls."

"What is this place called?" she asked.

"The tallgrass prairie."

"Interesting...and you say you can walk forever?"

"Forever, as long as it's with me. What say you, my soon-to-be bride...are you willing?"

"Am I willing? Yes, Adam, I'm a willing woman."

———

Don't miss out on your next favorite book!

Join the Melange Books mailing list at
www.melange-books.com/mail.html

THANK YOU FOR READING

Did you enjoy this book?

We invite you to leave a review at the website of your choice, such as Goodreads, Amazon, Barnes & Noble, etc.

DID YOU KNOW THAT LEAVING A REVIEW...

- Helps other readers find books they may enjoy.
- Gives you a chance to let your voice be heard.
- Gives authors recognition for their hard work.
- Doesn't have to be long. A sentence or two about why you liked the book will do.

ABOUT THE AUTHOR

Henry Hoffman is a former newspaper editor and public library director whose works have appeared in a variety of literary and trade publications, including the Library Journal, the Midwesterner, Encyclopedia of Library Science, America: History and Life, Historical Abstracts of the United States, the Cyclopedia of Literary Places, and the Encyclopedia of Natural Disasters. He is the author of five previous novels, including Bridge to Oblivion and The Veiled Lagoon, the first two entries in the  Adam Fraley mystery series. He is the recipient of the Florida Publishers Association's Gold Medal Award for Florida Fiction.

www.henryhoffman.net

ALSO BY HENRY HOFFMAN

with Melange Books